Heather MacQuarrie lives in Belfast, Northern Ireland, and also spends a good part of her time in southern Portugal. Happily married to Ross, they have two sons, two lovely daughters-in-law and one beautiful young granddaughter. Since leaving her teaching career behind in 2012 Heather has enjoyed reinventing herself as a writer of contemporary romance and mystery fiction.
Broken Cups is her fourth novel.

Also by Heather MacQuarrie

A Voice from the Past
In the Greater Scheme of Things
Blood is Thicker

www.heathermacquarrie.com

Thank you to:

Ross, for his unwavering support.
Clare, for her literary encouragement and critique.
Aaron and Jason, for their technical guidance.
The team at Troubador Publishing Ltd, especially Hannah and Sarah, for their professional services and friendly advice.
Everyone who continues to buy and read my books…

Many thanks to you all.

Broken Cups is a work of fiction and all the characters are purely a figment of my imagination. There is, however, a backdrop of reality in that some actual events of the late 80s and early 90s are mentioned in a diary. Whilst these events have nothing whatsoever to do with the story per se, I would like to acknowledge the sporting heroes of that era and pay tribute to all those who were affected by the devastating incidents that took place at Enniskillen, Warrington and Sheffield.

Heather xx

Heather MacQUARRIE

BROKEN CUPS

Matador
9 Priory Business Park,
Wistow Road, Kibworth Beauchamp,
Leicestershire. LE8 0RX
Tel: 0116 279 2299
Email: books@troubador.co.uk
Web: www.troubador.co.uk/matador
Twitter: @matadorbooks

ISBN 978 1785899 706

British Library Cataloguing in Publication Data.
A catalogue record for this book is available from the British Library.

Printed and bound in the UK by TJ International, Padstow, Cornwall
Typeset in 12pt Aldine401 BT by Troubador Publishing Ltd, Leicester, UK

Matador is an imprint of Troubador Publishing Ltd

Prologue

I saw them today. One minute I was jogging happily through the park admiring the beautiful autumn colours around me and believing that my nightmare was finally over; the next I was averting my gaze from the couple walking toward me, bold as brass, as though they hadn't a care in the world. They paid no attention to me as they strolled past, definitely didn't recognise me. But it was them all right. And they were pushing a pram. A blue pram with a blue fluffy blanket dangling over the edge and a blue quilt neatly tucked in around a little sleeping head donned in a blue hat. So they have a little boy. Maybe a couple of months old…

Chapter 1

"Hi Jillian, make yourself a cup of coffee. There are some of those caramel wafers that you like in the biscuit tin. I just need to finish this blogpost and I'll be right with you." Imogen waved her hand distractedly in the direction of her mother's state of the art kitchen as she continued to type her review, glancing at the notes she had scribbled whilst reading the book, which were now scattered across the table in front of her in no particular order. Jillian sighed. This was all becoming somewhat wearisome. She also was an avid reader, just like her friend, but the two of them approached the activity in such different ways nowadays. Pausing to give Toby an affectionate tickle, she headed towards the open door as directed. The playful Jack Russell padded behind her hoping for a treat.

Jillian never ceased to marvel at the opulence of her friend's home and couldn't help comparing it with her own parents' semi-detached house where she lived in much more modest surroundings despite her mother's almost obsessive attention to cleanliness and order.

Imogen's kitchen was pristine too, verging on the clinical with its shiny marble surfaces and bright white cupboard doors. Jillian admired the single orange gerbera in the quirky twisted glass vase and the pink orchid on the central island unit as she went over to the worktop in front of the huge picture window and turned on the coffee machine which burst into life with a spluttering of water and a loud tuneless noise. She selected a mug from a little carousel to the right of the machine and pushed the button for an Americano.

"Can I bring you one?" Jillian called out over the sound of the grinding coffee beans.

"Do I have time?"

"Not really. I've booked the appointment for five o'clock. We don't want to be late."

Imogen dropped her gaze to the clock in the corner of her screen. It was already a quarter past four. She saved the content she had just added but didn't activate it until she would have time to complete the article later. She and Jillian were due to view an apartment in a very sought after modern development in the east of the city; it would most certainly be snapped up by someone else if they failed to show up on time. She shut down her computer. "OK, let's go."

Jillian took a few sips of the hastily made hot drink and, snatching one bite of the biscuit, threw the rest to a delighted Toby who fell upon it with fervour, allowing the two girls to escape from the house without any fuss. Joanna would be home very soon anyway.

Jillian's car was the more accessible, blocking Imogen

in and taking up Joanna's space in the driveway, so they both scrambled in to her blue Yaris and she drove the short distance to what they hoped could soon become their new address. It was an exciting prospect, moving out of their respective parental homes and fending for themselves for the first time, even if they were staying within the suburbs of their native Belfast. At twenty-seven and twenty-eight many would have said the move was long overdue. Several of their friends were already married or at least living with a significant other. But neither Imogen nor Jillian had yet encountered that truly loving or lasting relationship. Boyfriends had come and gone, hopes had been raised and dashed, tears had been shed. It was time to move on; they couldn't live with their parents for ever.

"Did you ever read that book I bought you for Christmas?" Jillian now asked, her thoughts returning to the rushed coffee whilst Imogen was busy at her computer.

"Haven't had time. Sorry, I'll get round to it eventually." As she spoke, Imogen was checking her Twitter feed on her phone.

"It's October. You've had ten months."

"Have you seen the number of books I have to read?" She was now scrolling through her contacts, searching for a particular number. She found it and raised the phone to her ear. "Paulina, hi. It's me, Immy. I just saw your tweet. Sounds like a great book. See if you can get me a copy too...or did you read it electronically...you could just pass it on to me...oh that would be super... thanks."

Not for the first time Jillian began to wonder whether she was doing the right thing. Imogen had changed so much since she had become involved in this book blogging business. She had more time for her virtual friends, people she had never actually met, than for the fun activities they used to do together. They had known each other since the first day at grammar school when they had been thrown together simply because their surnames began with the same letter, Taylor-Scott and Tomlinson. Unwittingly that teacher had forged a friendship that had lasted right through the seven years of school, the four years of university and the ensuing five or so years of adulthood. They had been inseparable yet also receptive to the general camaraderie of the people around them.

"Paulina's book before mine then," Jillian said now, feeling a bit miffed.

Imogen put her phone back in her bag and stared at her friend somewhat hesitantly before replying. "What's the rush?" she then asked in a nonchalant tone. "I'm keeping yours for my next holiday when I can relax and enjoy it properly. It's only a book. It's not as if you wrote it yourself! People like Paulina and all the others are in touch with real authors and a whole community of bloggers who support each other. You should join in instead of being jealous. We all love it when someone new starts up a blog."

"No way!" Jillian retorted. "You won't find me signing up to anything of the sort. Those people are just a crowd of sycophants crawling all over each other with false praise and mock familiarity. It makes me sick."

Imogen recognised at once that there was a shred of truth in her friend's accusation but she was still shocked by the intensity of her remark. "Can we agree to disagree?" she proposed more pleasantly. "Let's concentrate on something more important. We're nearly at the flat and we don't want to come across as sworn enemies. The estate agent will picture us hurling crockery at the walls or screaming abuse at the neighbours."

They both giggled and any animosity was forgotten, temporarily at least. Jillian pulled into the small carpark and turned off the engine. And there was the estate agent standing by the neat flowerbed full of autumn geraniums in shades of pink, white and red, patiently waiting for them, a glossy brochure under his arm. Behind him the brown wooden door looked so inviting, beckoning them towards a new phase in their lives. Independence at last.

They were not disappointed. The accommodation looked even better than it had in the pictures they had seen on the website. Jillian found herself thinking that she could put up with her friend's new hobby after all if it meant getting to live in a place like this. She couldn't afford it on her own. Blogging, meanwhile, was the last thing on Imogen's mind. She was distracted by the two young men she saw on the stairwell as they entered the property. Did they live here too? What further incentive could she possibly need? They were hot; the taller guy in particular with his alluring smile and his designer stubble. She was already imagining herself cosying up with him after a tiring day at the office. He gave her a cheery greeting as he made his way down to his silver BMW which was parked just outside the door. His friend was handsome too but more reticent. Imogen noticed that he walked with a limp and appeared to have some communication difficulties. She looked forward to becoming acquainted with both of them. The two girls followed the agent into the ground-floor flat itself and wandered from room to room getting more excited by the minute. There was a bright and spacious lounge, a modern kitchen and bathroom and two well-proportioned bedrooms. It was perfect. In no time at all they had completed the tour and signed on the dotted line. The apartment was theirs; they could move in at the beginning of the month, which was just a week away.

"Can I have the front room?" Imogen made the request as Jillian drove her back home. "I'd like to be able to see my car from the window."

"That's fine with me," Jillian agreed. "I think I'd prefer the back room anyway. It might be quieter."

They smiled at each other. That was a painless enough decision. This was going to be fun.

Chapter 2

Joanna saw the car pulling up outside and opened the door to her daughter's friend before she even had time to ring the bell. "I've heard all about it," she told Jillian with a smile. "Sounds wonderful. I can't wait to see it for myself. Are your parents happy about the move?"

"They're ecstatic," Jillian replied, laughing. "They just need to get Vince to move on too and they'll have the place to themselves at last."

Joanna ignored the reference to Jillian's brother and simply directed the girl to the lounge where she said Imogen was relaxing. Jillian followed her in. "Wow! You're reading that book I gave you," she screeched with delight. "I thought you said you were too busy."

Imogen looked a bit embarrassed. "Sorry about that," she apologised. "I haven't been great company lately, have I? You started me thinking about it and I have to say I agree with you to some extent. The blog has taken over my life, turned me into some kind of a zombie. But that is all going to change from now on. I won't close it down altogether but I'm definitely going to spend less time chained to a computer screen or a phone." She waved the book in the air. "This is really good; I can hardly put it down." She looked pensive for a moment before adding, "I've had enough of reading books just because someone sends me a free copy and requests a review. Some of them are utter rubbish. But once I've accepted one and start reading it, I always feel that I have to go the whole distance. It's like GCSE English Lit all over again. Analysing every word, looking for hidden meanings, taking notes, trying to think of something positive to say even when you hate it. Whatever happened to reading for reading's sake and just enjoying it?"

Jillian was speechless. How wonderful to have her best friend back, saying the things that she herself had been thinking all along. Jillian liked nothing better than pausing by the book stand in Sainsbury's and popping a novel into her trolley of groceries or browsing in Waterstones, choosing something for the weekend or for her holidays. Yet she knew that Imogen had discovered some brilliant books that had never made it to the shelves in those stores; there must be a happy medium.

"I'm going to make my blog much more general," Imogen was now saying. "Instead of books, books, books it will be more of an online diary about life in general. And I'm going to limit myself to an hour a day, or a maximum of two when there's something of particular interest. If I review a book it will be because I just happened to come across that book and enjoyed it. No more pandering to people or begging publishers for advance copies."

"Well good for you!" Jillian exclaimed. "Isn't that what 'blog' means anyway. A 'log' is a diary and a 'weblog' is a diary on the 'web', 'blog' for short."

"Really? I never really thought about it," Imogen mused, impressed as usual with Jillian's knowledge of words. She was like a walking thesaurus at times.

"I used to keep a diary," Joanna now chipped in, having overheard the latter part of the girls' conversation. "A lot of girls did in my day. It started out as a teenage craze but I kept mine going into my thirties! I found writing things down could be quite therapeutic. I suppose that's where Imogen gets it from. Runs in the family."

"What sort of things did you write about?" Jillian asked, smiling at her friend's mother.

"Anything and everything," she answered. "When I was younger it was mostly just an account of how I spent my time but as I got older I used to write more about my thoughts and feelings and sometimes added things like favourite recipes and the like or something that was on the 'News'."

"It would be fascinating to see some of them and compare them to the sort of blogs that are around today. Did you keep them?"

Joanna laughed. "I did keep some but I wouldn't dare show them to you. Everything is so public nowadays with people posting selfies and personal information all over the social media networks. It was different in our day. Diaries were private; I had a few five year ones that even came with a little padlock and key. No-one was ever allowed to see what I had written."

"Did you write about meeting Dad?" Imogen's imagination started to run wild. "Getting married? Becoming pregnant? Me being born?"

"Yes," Joanna revealed. "That was all documented."

"Oh, you have to let me see that! Come on, it's part of my history."

Joanna hesitated. "I don't know. I'd have to reread it myself first to check that's it's not too cringeworthy! Like I said, my diaries were private; for my eyes only."

"I wonder whether my mum kept a diary when I was born," Jillian now speculated. "That would make interesting reading too."

Imogen brought the conversation back to the matter in hand, showing her friend a list she had started to compile, consisting of essential items they would need to gather up or purchase within the next few days. Jillian scanned it and immediately added a few more of her own. This was going to be expensive.

"We can probably get everything in IKEA," Jillian remarked. "Enough to get us started at least."

"What's that you're adding?" Imogen asked her as she saw the pencil making another scribble on the page.

"Pillows," Jillian told her. "You've got pillow cases listed but nothing to put them on."

Imogen laughed. "Well spotted," she agreed. "At least I did include the beds themselves. I certainly wouldn't fancy sleeping without a pillow."

"I suppose it just shows how much we've taken for granted living at home," Jillian observed.

"Just what I was thinking," Joanna chortled, nodding

her head in agreement. "You're going to get your eyes opened now and no mistake."

Imogen handed her the sheet of paper. "Can you see any other glaring omissions, Mum?" she asked.

Joanna cast her eye over the list. "Well," she prompted, after pondering for a moment, "you've got a kettle, a toaster and an iron."

"What's wrong with that? We can add other electrical appliances at a later date. Surely those are the three basics."

"Yes, but how are you going to use the iron?"

This was met with a blank stare from both girls so Joanna did a little mime with her right arm until Jillian twigged. "Ah! An ironing board." It was added to the ever-growing list.

"We should have got married," Imogen joked, "and then people would have bought us all these things."

As they continued to chat about the events of the day and the preparations they would need to make before moving into their new apartment, they were both quite unaware that they had just opened a can of worms which would have far-reaching consequences for all of them. Joanna's secret diaries might reveal more than they bargained for.

Chapter 3

Bradley Harrington could hardly believe his luck. Those two girls he had seen viewing the building were moving into the downstairs apartment. He observed them from his bay window, taking in their poise and elegance which was so apparent, even dressed as they were in baggy tracksuits. The taller one was particularly beautiful. Her reddish-brown hair tumbled over her shoulders in a mass of sleek, gentle curls, framing an oval-shaped face with big round eyes and a friendly smile. Her friend, slightly smaller in stature, had almost black glossy hair, cut in a neat bob. They both looked quite athletic. How pleasant it would be having these two as neighbours though to be honest, he surmised, anyone would be preferable to that pompous bank manager who had recently moved out. Bradley found himself wondering what the two girls did for a living. Well, no time like the present, he decided. He would go down and introduce himself, see if they needed any help.

Just as he reached the bottom of the stairs, the front door opened and Bradley came face to face with the new arrivals. They were each carrying three or four large bags.

"Hi," he greeted them with a smile, "can I help you with those? I'm Bradley by the way. I live upstairs."

"Imogen," said Imogen, accepting his offer and handing over her belongings. "And this is Jillian. Thanks a lot. That's very kind of you."

"Pleased to meet you," added Jillian. "We're moving in on Monday but just thought we'd start leaving off some of our stuff. We have a few items of furniture arriving tomorrow."

Imogen unlocked the door and all three entered the ground-floor flat which was as yet devoid of tables, chairs, beds or anything else. But it was newly painted and had a fresh, airy feel about it.

"Why don't you come up for a coffee when you've finished," Bradley suggested, setting Imogen's bags on the polished wooden floor. "If we're going to be neighbours we might as well exchange a few details."

The blood started to pump through Imogen's veins at a very much accelerated pace. "Thanks," she said, attempting to hide her excitement. "That would be lovely. We haven't even got a kettle yet or any mugs."

"This is mainly clothes," Jillian added, pointing to the bulging bags. "A coffee would be great."

"Right, just come on up when it suits," Bradley told them. "I'll be in all evening." He went back upstairs and took a look around his own living space. It was pretty tidy but he wanted to impress. He plumped up the blue and grey cushions and arranged the papers on his corner unit into a neat pile, setting his pen and stapler on top.

A couple of used mugs and plates were removed to the kitchen. Finally he checked the bathroom, just in case, adding a fresh towel and a new toilet roll. Then he sat down and turned on the television. Scrolling through the channels he selected a random documentary about Spanish architecture, which he was half-heartedly watching when he heard the expected rap at the door. "Come on in girls, you're very welcome," he said in greeting, turning off the TV and throwing the door open. They both stepped inside and were immediately aware of a pleasant homely atmosphere, fresh and uncluttered without being minimalist.

"So are you on your own this evening?" Imogen asked, looking around for the other guy they had spotted before. "I presume that was your flat-mate we saw earlier in the week."

"No, Alastair doesn't live here," Bradley replied with a grin. "He was just visiting. I was about to leave him home when we met the two of you that day. He doesn't drive himself."

"Gosh, that must make life difficult for him," remarked Jillian. "I'd feel trapped without my car."

"Is it because of his limp?" Imogen added. "We couldn't help noticing."

"Yes, partly that," Bradley confirmed. "Alastair suffered some brain damage as a child. He's made great strides but his reactions are still a bit too slow for safe driving." He pointed towards the brown leather sofa, inviting his new neighbours to sit down. "I'll just go and make that coffee."

"This is nice," Jillian observed, casting an approving eye around the tastefully furnished room. "And he seems very friendly."

"Not to say sexy," trilled Imogen.

The coffee arrived with a selection of biscuits on a plate. "So tell me a bit about yourselves," Bradley began. "What brings you to this part of town? Do you work nearby? How long have you known each other?" Once again he admired Jillian's long wavy hair as he spoke and aimed his questions mainly in her direction but it was Imogen who answered him first.

"We've known each other since schooldays," she said cheerfully. "We're just good friends." She wanted to make it clear right from the start that they were not lesbians, just in case there was any confusion on that score. She saw Bradley relax. So he *had* been fishing for that information. Now she just needed the same declaration from him. "I'm a personal trainer," she told him. "I'm not based in any particular gym but meet my clients in various locations depending on where they have their own memberships. And I also give talks about nutrition and healthy life-style to groups of people, both adults and children."

"Ah," rejoined Bradley, "hence the tracksuits. Are you both in that line of work?"

Once again it was Imogen who jumped in first. "No, not at all. We're only in this comfortable gear today for moving stuff about. I actually have an office job for a good part of the time, planning talks and organising timetables and Jillian's not really into sport at all. She has a much more glamorous job."

15

Bradley turned his attention to Jillian. His head wasn't often turned by a pretty woman he had just met but there was something about her, something instinctive that he couldn't explain. He gave her a warm smile. "So tell me about your glamorous job," he invited. "I bet you're a model or an actress."

Jillian laughed. "Nothing like that," she declared. "I'm the editor of a magazine. It's called 'All in a Day's Work'. I interview people about their occupations, looking for quirky little details that the general public mightn't know about and also probe for ideas to help my readers achieve a good work/life balance."

"I've seen that in the shops!" exclaimed Bradley. "I remember flicking through a copy a few months back. It was mostly about farming."

"And you didn't buy it!" retorted Jillian with jocular accusation. "Yes, I had good fun producing that issue. I was knee deep in mud one day and even had a ride on a tractor. So don't believe my friend here when she calls it glamorous."

"So you do that sort of thing yourself even though you're the editor?"

"Yes, I have a whole month to work on each issue but I do have an assistant, a young fellow called Ben, which is good because he makes sure I don't see everything purely from a female point of view."

"I love the way you call him a 'young' fellow," Bradley grinned. "You're not exactly old yourself."

"Ah, but he's only nineteen. He was still at school a couple of years ago. He's quite mature for his age and a real whizz kid on the computer."

Imogen broke into the conversation again. "So what do you do, Bradley?"

"Company Director," he stated in a matter-of-fact tone. "You may have heard of my firm, H & C Security. Well, I'm the 'H' half of it. Bradley Harrington. The 'C' stands for my partner, Nigel Cunningham, and Nigel's wife is our receptionist-cum -secretary."

"Security? Wow! That's useful to have upstairs. We've moved to the right place," Imogen replied. "So what does it actually involve?"

"Fitting and maintaining locks and burglar alarms is our main function. We do private homes and also quite a few shops and other public buildings. In addition we run an advisory service, informing people about other safety measures like shatterproof glass, smoke alarms and carbon monoxide detectors for example." He spoke with an air of pride and rightly so. He and Nigel had set up the business from scratch and it had gone from strength to strength.

"You have some super photographs," Jillian observed, standing up and going over to view more closely the large frameless images on the walls. There was one of a couple of dogs against a backdrop of a very picturesque mountain scene obviously taken in the Mournes and another of Bradley himself with an older woman walking on the sand and shingle beach at Portballintrae. "Is that your mum?"

"Yes," Bradley replied, "and those are the family pets, Bruno and Jasper."

"They're very striking photos. They look really professional."

Bradley smiled. "My dad will be glad to hear that," he divulged. "It's what he does for a living."

"He's a professional photographer?"

"Yes."

"And what about your mum?" Imogen asked. "What does she do?"

"She runs a catering firm, organising the food and drinks for private functions."

"So is that how they met? She was doing the food and he was taking the photographs?"

"It's not actually. They met years ago before either of them were in those jobs. But it is handy. They can often work together and help to promote each other."

"Sounds ideal."

By the time they had finished their coffee the three of them had exchanged quite a lot of information about each other. Bradley told the girls a bit more about his friend, Alastair. He had met him some years ago when they were still at school. Due to his learning difficulties, Alastair had attended a special school and Bradley's college had organised a scheme as part of their 'personal development and mutual understanding' curriculum, whereby pupils were encouraged to interact with those who were disadvantaged in some way. Bradley and Alastair had become 'buddies' through this scheme and their friendship had survived even after they moved on. They didn't see each other so often nowadays but there was still a close bond between them.

"What a lovely story," Jillian said with admiration. "I'm sure most of the other pupils only took part in the scheme because they had to and just paid lip service to it."

"What does Alastair do?" Imogen asked. "Is he able to work?"

"Yes, he has a job in a garden centre. He's brilliant with plants."

"Oh, that's wonderful. Was he born with his disability or did he develop it through some illness? You said something about brain damage." Imogen too applauded the way Bradley had forged a real friendship with his school 'buddy'.

Bradley revealed that Alastair had been involved in an accident when he was just five years old. His leg had been mangled resulting in several operations over the years. Now he just had a slight limp which hopefully would disappear following his current course of intensive physiotherapy. The simultaneous head injury had caused a slowness in speech and action. "His father was killed in the same incident," he concluded.

"Oh that's awful," said both girls in unison.

There was a respectful silence for a few moments before they returned to happier topics of conversation and ended up swapping phone numbers, email addresses and Twitter contacts. Bradley had been feeling a bit down recently, since breaking up with his girlfriend, Della. It would be very nice having such an affable pair living downstairs. Especially Jillian. Jillian was gorgeous. He wondered whether she had a boyfriend.

Chapter 4

Two days passed in a flurry of activity with Imogen's dad, Keith and Jillian's dad, Robert helping out with any heavy lifting, Robert one day and Keith the next. Keith was the Managing Director of a kitchen design company and Robert worked as a sound engineer in the film and television industry. They never seemed to be both available at the same time. Even though the two girls had been close for so many years the two families did not socialise together but each had their own circle of friends. In the end they had given up trying to get their parents together. But both dads had been helpful in their own way and Jillian's brother, Vincent had also got involved, hanging curtains for them in their lounge and bedrooms. The furniture they had chosen had arrived as promised. The whole place was taking shape nicely, starting to look like a real home.

"Thanks for everything," Imogen said, giving her dad a hug. He was the last to leave after helping to assemble some flat pack wardrobes.

"No problem," Keith assured her as he got into his

car. "The house is going to seem very quiet without you. But we're glad you're not moving too far away." He started up the engine and began to reverse out of the parking space, then stopped and rolled down the window. Lifting something from the door pocket he addressed his daughter again. "Oh, I nearly forgot. Your mother sent this over. She says you're to take good care of it. She wants it back in one piece."

Imogen glanced at the book he was handing her. It was one of her mother's diaries! Quickly she checked the date – 1987, the year of her own birth. Wow! Joanna was really going to let her read this. She could hardly wait to get started.

"Thanks, Dad," she called after the moving car. "This should be interesting."

Back inside, Imogen placed the diary by her bedside and stood back to survey the transformation of her room. No longer an empty shell, it now had a double bed draped in turquoise and lilac, a small chest of drawers and a range of wardrobes and shelves along one wall. On the floor there were two scatter rugs in a deeper shade of purple. She sighed with contentment and started to hang up some of her clothes. Jillian was in her own room, also starting to tidy things away. She had opted for hues of powder blue and pink and was delighted with the effect. They both heard the doorbell and emerged from their respective rooms at the same time. Imogen opened the door and there stood Bradley, a bottle of Champagne in his hand.

"House-warming present," he said, handing over the

gift. "Now what are you two doing for dinner? You won't be wanting to cook on your first night."

"We were just going to order a pizza," Jillian said gaily. "There wasn't much time for shopping today but we have stocked up with the basics so we can do breakfast in the morning; bread and milk, coffee, butter, marmalade and a few yoghurts." She pointed towards the bottle of Champagne. "Thanks for this. That's really kind of you."

"I can offer you a stir-fry if you like. Nothing fancy – just chicken with onions and peppers, a bit of chilli and garlic."

The girls glanced at each other and nodded. "That sounds wonderful," gushed Imogen.

"OK, shall we say eight o'clock?"

"Perfect. We'll bring this with us and you can help us drink it."

"He's nearly too good to be true," Jillian sighed as she closed the door again. "We've certainly landed on our feet." She knew that Imogen had been swooning over him since they first met but she also was very attracted to their new neighbour. Hopefully things wouldn't get awkward on that score. They went back to organising their belongings and then freshened up before heading upstairs.

A delicious aroma of onions, garlic and herbs wafted out as Bradley opened the door and once again welcomed them to his home. Imogen handed him back the bottle he had given them and popping the cork, he straightaway poured some into the three flutes he had sitting ready on the table. They each took a sip of the sparkling liquid.

Lovely. Declining their offer of assistance Bradley told the girls to make themselves comfortable while he returned to the kitchen to put the finishing touches to his recipe. A dash of red wine, a little more seasoning and a bowl of fluffy white rice on the side. In no time at all the three of them were sitting down enjoying the delicious meal he had prepared. When Bradley revealed that he used to cook for his former girlfriend from whom he had recently split, Imogen and Jillian alike breathed a sigh of relief, both secretly thinking the same thing. *He is straight and he is unattached.* They chatted like old friends, enjoying the free and easy atmosphere, but left soon afterwards. It had been a tiring day and there was still much to be done.

Back in their own kitchen, Imogen unpacked the new crockery, glasses, cutlery and pans they had bought during the week and started to wash each item while Jillian wiped all the cupboards, inside and out.

"I knew we'd forget something," said Imogen as she realised they had no tea towels and added them to a new list.

"Never mind," Jillian answered, "they'll be dry in the morning. We also need a pair of scissors and a tin opener. Let's call it a day. I'm exhausted."

And they were both tired, but elated at the same time. It was fun starting out on their own, the beginning of a new adventure.

Imogen always found it hard to get to sleep on her first night in a new place, like when she stayed in a foreign hotel on holiday, and this was no different. She lay awake listening to the unfamiliar sounds and peeping out through the curtains every now and then to check that her red Audi was still safely parked opposite the window. The traffic on the main road could be heard making a constant humming sound which was so unlike the silence of the cul-de-sac where she had lived with her parents. She knew that it was just a case of getting used to it. The bed also felt strange. It was perfectly comfortable but different and she couldn't sleep in spite of the tiredness. After a while she picked up her mother's diary and started to leaf through it. There appeared to be an entry for every single day, some very brief, some much longer, some neatly written, some hastily scrawled. Gingerly she turned to the page for 20th October, the date of her own birth.

My baby arrived today and it's a girl. She is so gorgeous and my heart is just bursting with love. I've never felt pain like it in my life but Keith stayed with me the whole time and made it bearable. He is the best husband a girl could have. I am so lucky.

Tears came to her eyes as Imogen read those words, written twenty-eight years ago. She turned to the next page.

Imogen. We're going to call her Imogen. She has lovely blue eyes and a shock of jet black hair, just like her daddy. She kept me awake most of the night but I don't care. I just love holding her in my arms and cuddling her. When she's in the cot I keep staring at her to check she is still breathing! Keith brought me some lovely flowers. Mum and dad came to see her. They are the proudest grandparents ever.

Imogen's maternal grandparents were in their eighties now and still in relatively good health. They had always taken an active interest in her life and had followed all her efforts and achievements with pride. She looked forward to showing them around her new home. Unfortunately her paternal grandparents had both passed away within the last few years and Keith was only now getting used to life without them. They had also been lovely people who had enriched Imogen's childhood enormously. She turned the page and found a reference to them.

Annie and Don came round to see their new granddaughter. They brought me some gorgeous Babygros and bibs and a teddy bear that used to be Keith's. He was really excited to see it again; he had no idea that they had kept it.

It was wonderful reading about the first few days of her life. So much happiness and joy. Tentatively Imogen counted back. It must have been about January. She skimmed through the pages and found several entries that took her breath away.

Keith and I have never been so close. Now that we've stopped taking precautions our intimacy is so much more intense. I love him so much.

So no doubt that she was a planned baby. That gave her a warm feeling of happiness. She snuggled into the crisp new duvet wanting more.

I feel sure that it must have happened last night. We made love twice and somehow it seemed even more special than usual. How wonderful it would be if we really have created a new life.

Wow! That's me she's talking about. She must have been right because the dates tally nicely. And she really, really wanted me. I'm so glad that she allowed me to read this. Imogen felt quite overwhelmed.

And then at the beginning of February:

I'm pregnant!!! The doctor confirmed it this morning. I haven't told Keith yet – I'll do that in bed tonight. He will be over the moon!

Imogen was glad that Joanna had not gone into specific detail regarding her sex life. These were her parents, after all. Too much information would have been a bit embarrassing. No doubt her mother had vetted it by checking back herself and making sure there was nothing inappropriate before agreeing to hand it over. And it was no wonder that she wanted it back. It must be wonderful to have such a personal record of the important events in your life. She skipped forward to the end of the book and read about her first Christmas, what a joyful occasion it had been for the whole family. Imogen sighed with contentment. As she lay back on her new pillow and surveyed the transformation of her bedroom from the bare shell it had been just a couple of days ago, it struck her that the old ways were often the best. She should really make a few notes herself. In her own handwriting. Something she could look back on in the future. Maybe even show to her own daughter some day.

As she leafed through the diary again she noticed that Joanna had also mentioned several items of world news, mainly sports events that she had watched on television. She learnt that Nigel Mansell had won the Formula 1 British Grand Prix but that he had crashed with Ayrton Senna in the first lap of the Belgian race. The World Champion Athletics had been held in Rome and New Zealand had won the Rugby World Cup. No wonder Imogen herself had turned out to be so sporty. On a sad note she read that a bomb had gone off in Enniskillen. Imogen had heard about that dreadful incident from documentaries about the 'troubles' and she had been to the beautiful town of Enniskillen and visited the nearby caves where she had seen amazing examples of stalactites and stalagmites. She had also enjoyed a boat trip on Lough Erne, just outside the town. Seeing what her mum had written about the events of 1987 brought that sad event in history to life.

As she closed the book and turned out the light, Imogen suddenly realised that she hadn't returned to her own blog since the conversation with Jillian, nor had she read anyone else's. And she hadn't missed it. She had been far too busy enjoying real life. She fell asleep at last, happy in the knowledge that her parents were, and always had been, a truly loving couple and hoping that life would soon take her in the same direction. She drifted into a semi-conscious dream.

It must be an awesome feeling, finding out that you are pregnant, knowing that you are going to bring a new life into the world. I hope it happens to me soon. I would so love to be a mother. I have been disappointed so many times. I really thought Sam loved me. I pictured us sharing a home and having a family together. Until Holly came on the scene. Then there was Kyle. That didn't work out either. Josh and Martin. Maybe Bradley will turn out to be the one. Or maybe my knight in shining armour is somewhere around the corner, just waiting to be discovered. I wonder whether Sam and Holly are still together. I still miss him.

Chapter 5

Bradley was staring absent-mindedly through the window one evening, about two weeks after the girls had moved in downstairs, when he suddenly became aware of Imogen's car leaving the carpark. She seemed to be on her own. Jillian's Yaris was still parked beside his own BMW. Was it too soon to make a move? He had started to think about Jillian a lot. And after the day he had just endured, a little time spent in her company would be a lovely distraction. He grabbed a bottle of Pinot Grigio from the fridge and hurried down the stairs before he would take cold feet. He rang the bell.

"Oh, hi Bradley," Jillian greeted him with a smile.

He held up the bottle. "Fancy joining me in a glass of wine? I need to unwind. It's been a hard day."

Jillian laughed. "Oh dear," she uttered. "Come on in and tell me all about it. A glass of wine would be great. Imogen's gone over to see her parents but hopefully I can be a good listener on my own." She pointed towards her new burgundy-coloured sofa, inviting him to have a seat, and went to fetch a couple of glasses. Bradley then poured the wine. "So tell me about your day," Jillian began.

"I could definitely give you some material for your magazine," he replied with a sigh of exasperation. "You said that you write about aspects of the job that people might not have imagined…"

Jillian looked interested. "I could certainly add you to my list for an interview," she returned, "especially if you have something juicy."

Bradley began to salivate at her choice of words. He could come up with something juicy all right but it would have nothing to do with work. He paused for a moment to control his feelings. "I had an appointment at a private residence today," he then revealed. "I won't say where it was due to client confidentiality but it was horrendous." Jillian raised her eyebrows, waiting for him to elaborate. "The house was filthy," Bradley continued. "Most people go the extra mile to make sure their premises are spic and span when they have booked an appointment with us. There isn't a thing in disarray. They realise that we will be all over the house, checking the most appropriate positions for sensors and so on. But this couple today had not even tidied up let alone cleaned the place. The smell hit me as soon as I went through the door. There was dirty laundry all over the furniture and uneaten food on greasy plates in at least three of the rooms. It was a big house. They obviously have plenty of money." He shuddered at the memory of the inexcusable squalor. "I couldn't even describe the state of the bathroom and toilet and I actually saw a mouse scuttling across the floor in one of the bedrooms," he said in conclusion.

Jillian was horrified. "Have people no shame?" she protested. "You should have walked out and refused to do the job."

"I did consider it," he answered, "and you're probably right. The first thing I did when I got home was strip off and get into the shower."

Jillian took a deep breath. He did smell delicious and the thought of him standing naked under the shower was quite erotic. It was her turn to attempt to keep her feelings under control. She only succeeded by directing the conversation away from him and talking about her own day at work. She was collaborating with an architect this week, she told him, and had spent the day poring over plans for a new housing development. She could hardly believe the amount of time and energy that went in to deciding where power points should be located. And light fittings. "I just take these things for granted," she professed. "I arrange the furniture and fittings according to what sockets are available but it seems that it should be the other way round."

They ended up looking around the room and deciding whether good decisions had been made when the layout of the girls' apartment was in the planning stage. One particular socket was definitely overloaded with cables supplying four different appliances all plugged in to an extension lead behind the sofa, yet another was not in use at all due to its position right beside the door. Bradley pointed this out but mentioned that the latter was useful for things like a vacuum cleaner. He added, however, that the design offered limited choice in deciding where to position the sofa. Some people might have preferred it in front of the window but that would have resulted in all those cables being exposed. Working in the security business, Bradley was well used to analysing such issues.

"Imogen would have enjoyed this conversation," Jillian suddenly remarked. "She was complaining yesterday that there wasn't a suitable power point for plugging in her hair dryer. And she would have loved that story about the mouse! She'll be sorry to have missed you."

Bradley didn't want to talk about Imogen. She was a nice enough girl but it was Jillian he was interested in. He ignored the comment and brought the conversation round to the items he could see on the shelves around them. "I have this CD too," he said, picking up the latest album by Ed Sheeran.

"You have good taste in music then," Jillian declared. "Who else do you like?"

"Much the same as you by the look of things." He fingered a few other CDs on the shelf and then picked up a book. "Are you reading this?" he asked.

"Yes," replied Jillian. "I love Maggie O'Farrell's novels. This one is really intriguing. I've nearly finished it as you can see." There was a red bookmark sticking out from between the pages, not far from the back cover. "What about you? Are you a reader?"

"When I have time, yes. I like thrillers and mysteries."

A box set of DVDs caught his eye next. "So you're a *Morse* fan," he remarked.

"Brilliant series," agreed Jillian, "especially when you link it with *Endeavour* and *Lewis* and watch it all in sequence." She watched Bradley pick up a photograph next. Was it her imagination or was he stalling for time? Maybe he was hoping that Imogen would soon be back.

"Who's this?" he asked.

"That's Imogen's parents, Joanna and Keith. Joanna sells ladies' fashion and Keith designs kitchens."

"Any brothers or sisters?"

"No, she's an only child. But they have a Jack Russell called Toby."

"And what about you?"

"One brother, Vincent." She looked around and found a photograph of her own family. "That's Vince with my dad, Robert." She lifted another one. "And that's my mum, Dorothy. She's a writer."

"Really? What sort of writing does she do?"

"She's published several short stories and a series of picture books for young children."

They were now standing close to the door and Bradley looked at his watch. Then he smiled at Jillian and looked as though he was about to say something but she spoke first suggesting that he might want to have another drink while they waited for Imogen. She should be home very soon.

Bradley looked a bit guilty. "I should be honest," he confessed. "I knew she wasn't here. I saw her leaving." He hesitated. "That's why I came down."

Their eyes met and words became unnecessary. Bradley touched her lightly on the cheek, then ran his hand gently through her long wavy hair. Jillian made no attempt to stop him. She responded by moving closer and placing her own hand on the nape of his neck and fingering his short, dark hair. "I'm glad you did," she whispered. And suddenly they were kissing and kissing and kissing, clinging to each other with a passion that surprised them both. "You're beautiful," Bradley murmured, his breath tickling her ear when the kiss finally came to an end. "Can we do this again sometime soon?"

"You'd better believe it," Jillian responded with a seductive smile. "I'll be counting on it." Then she accompanied him to the door where they kissed again before he went upstairs. Jillian sat down and took a deep breath. She felt a surge of happiness coupled with a tinge of apprehension, knowing that Imogen had her sights firmly set on pulling Bradley for herself. She wouldn't say anything yet. It had only been a kiss, after all. But what a kiss! She licked her lips, savouring the memory, and then jumped up to hide the evidence. Hastily secreting the rest of the wine at the back of the fridge, she washed the glasses and returned them to the cupboard just as her friend arrived home.

"Mum gave me another diary to read," Imogen said eagerly. "I'm whacked so I'm just going to lie down and make a start on it, see what I was like as a four-year-old!"

"OK, see you in the morning." Jillian's heart was still racing. She was relieved that she wouldn't have to account for her evening. She would simply go to bed herself and finish her novel. And dream of things to come. Hopefully.

***

A quick flick through the 1991 diary once again revealed Joanna's interest in sport. Imogen learnt that Michael Stich had won the men's Wimbledon final with the women's title going to Steffi Graf, although all the other major tournaments that year had been won by Monica Seles. France had beaten America in the Davis Cup and John Parrott was the world snooker champion. Gosh, her mother was a mine of information. Next she noticed a reference to the first visit of the Tall Ships to Belfast. She had a very vague recollection of going to view the ships with her parents, mainly because she had seen photographs of herself at the event in some of the family albums. She didn't recall most of the things she was reading about. After all she was only three, four in October. She turned to the date of her birthday.

Imogen is four. I can hardly believe how the time has flown. We had a party for her – just the family and wee Jimmy from next door. I think her favourite present was the tub of bubbles that his mum brought. She got more fun out of that than from all her other expensive gifts put together. We could have saved a fortune. Mum made her a cake and she loved blowing out the candles. We had to re-light them umpteen times.

Imogen smiled. She remembered Jimmy but hadn't thought about him for years. She used to love going to play in his garden because he had a swing and he used to come to hers because there was plenty of room to kick a football. His family had gone to live in England when the two of them were about ten. He could be anywhere now. Maybe he has a Facebook or Twitter account – something to check out later. She found another reference to herself.

Spent most of the day doing jigsaws with Imogen. She's getting quite good at finding the right piece and fitting it in, as long as there are no more than ten or twelve in total. Hopefully tomorrow will be a better day so we can get outside and maybe go to the park. Rained all day. Annie's going to babysit tomorrow night so Keith and I can get a night out – a rare luxury these days.

There were plenty more entries like that, pretty mundane ordinary occurrences typical of any young mother bringing up a child. The pages were full of visits to the doctor, minor accidents and so on mingled with games they had played and TV programmes they had watched together. *Sesame Street* had been their favourite. But suddenly Imogen's eyes were drawn to something quite different.

It's been a whole year. I still can't quite believe that it happened. We never talk about it but I still feel so ashamed. Keith has bottled up his guilt too. We're trying to forget but it's just not the same any more. Some of the magic has gone and I doubt whether we can ever get it back. I keep thinking about that little boy and his daddy.

Imogen blinked and glanced at the top of the page – 10th November. That would have been a few weeks after her fourth birthday. She racked her brains but had no recollection of anything that could explain her mother's words. And she realised now that the warmth of her parents' loving relationship which had shone through in the 1987 diary was not so evident in this book. Keith was not mentioned as much and when he was it was simply cold, hard facts about something they had done together. Whilst it was true that she never said a word against him and there was evidence of a few nights out at the cinema or for a meal, where was the passion? Joanna and Keith were still together now in 2015 and Imogen had never doubted that their marriage was rock-solid. All couples went through bad patches from time to time, she told herself. Did one of them have an affair? Somehow that didn't ring true. There was only one thing for it; she would have to get her hands on the 1990 diary. With a sigh Imogen set the current book aside and reluctantly went to sleep.

Chapter 6

As the beautiful Indian summer began to fade into the colder, darker, misty days of November, Imogen and Jillian both began to feel more and more at home in their new accommodation. They took turns to cook and to clean and soon became accustomed to each other's little quirks and habits. Jillian was the tidier of the two and was forever straightening up cushions and polishing surfaces whilst Imogen spent hours glued to her computer screen oblivious to the state of the room around her. She was trying hard to stick to her new resolution but blogging had become so much a part of her life that she was finding it difficult to adjust. Her Twitter profile, however, no longer invited people to follow @immysbookcase but instead had been renamed @immyswindowonlife; she had been true to her word in making her posts and tweets much more general and varied. Jillian was delighted to see that her friend had at least made an effort to break free from the clutches of Paulina and the others so she was quite content, for the time being, to put up with her lack of assistance with the daily chores.

Glancing out though the window now, Jillian spotted the gardener removing what remained of the geraniums and planting some daffodil and tulip bulbs in their place, adding a few winter pansies around the edges to give some interim colour. She could just imagine the lovely display they would have in the springtime. The older woman who lived in the adjoining flat was chatting to the gardener as he worked. She was a bit of a mystery to the girls as were the two young men who lived above her apartment. They all kept very much to themselves and had barely muttered a greeting as their paths crossed on the way in or out. Bradley was still the only other occupant of the building that they had got to know.

"Are you in or out tonight?" Imogen asked her as she breezed into the room, her phone in one hand and a cup of coffee in the other. "I thought we could invite Bradley down for supper. I could do a curry or something."

Jillian had still not told her friend that she and Bradley had kissed, and not just once. There had been a second opportunity one day last week when they had both arrived home from work about the same time and they had both seized that opportunity with relish. She should really come clean about it. But Imogen was looking excited at the prospect and waiting for an answer. She cleared her throat with a little cough. "A curry would be lovely," she proclaimed at last, "but I'm pretty sure Bradley said he was busy tonight."

"Oh." Imogen looked disappointed but immediately accepted that Jillian must have bumped into him and obtained this information. "Never mind. Some other time. I'll do the curry anyway. It's my turn to cook."

The gardener was now getting into his van and the older lady had moved away. Bradley suddenly appeared beside his car and, spotting Jillian at the window, gave her a friendly wave. Jillian straightaway dashed into the foyer and out the front door. "You're busy tonight," she hissed in his ear.

"I am?"

"Well, just pretend you are. That's what I told Imogen. She was going to ask you down for supper but I put her off. It's a bit awkward, the three of us together. Just until I tell her about us. Please!"

Bradley grinned. "Tell her what?" he asked teasingly.

"Good question," echoed Imogen who had followed her friend out and slipped up behind them unnoticed. "What's going on?" When nobody answered she immediately realised that she knew the answer to her own question. It was pretty obvious what was going on. Bradley was looking somewhat sheepish and Jillian's face was flushed bright red. But still neither of them spoke. Imogen turned on her heel and went back indoors. It was several minutes before they joined her. They came into the lounge holding hands.

"Sorry, Imogen," Jillian began. "I was trying to find a way to tell you but …"

Imogen interrupted her. "It's OK. I should have realised. Blind as a bat."

This was followed by an awkward silence.

"Any chance I'm still invited for that curry?" quizzed Bradley after a moment.

The two girls looked at each other and smiled. "Yes, of course," Imogen said, happy to clear the air, "as long as you two can behave yourselves around me."

"You don't mind?" Jillian whispered as she let go of Bradley's hand and led her friend into the kitchen where they could talk alone.

"I mind being kept in the dark and made to look a fool," Imogen answered, "but I don't mind the two of you hooking up. It's not as if you stole him from me. He was never mine in the first place." She had a sudden flashback.

It's nothing like the last time. Nothing like the humiliation and hurt I felt when Sam told me he wanted to be with Holly. Sam was mine. We had a future together. Or so I thought.

"Sorry. It just happened. Not that anything much *has* happened. We just kissed a couple of times. But I think he really likes me and I …"

"Spare me the details. I can put two and two together for myself."

"So you're really OK for tonight?"

"Yes. I'm happy for you." She gave her friend a hug. "You deserve him, Jillian. You'll make a lovely couple."

"Hey, we're not getting married or anything! It's just been a couple of kisses so far but I do think it could be leading somewhere. It's early days."

"Well get back in there before he disappears on you. I'll just make a note of what I need for my recipe."

Jillian returned to the lounge and joined Bradley on the sofa where they shared another kiss. And another. And as their eyes finally met, they both knew instinctively that they wanted more from each other. At least it was out in the open now. What they didn't know, however, was that in accepting Imogen's supper invitation, they had unwittingly created an opportunity for her; they had just opened a door which would lead to Imogen also finding the potential love of her life.

★★★

The supermarket was particularly busy that afternoon. The pumpkins, apple tarts and scary costumes had disappeared for another year and the aisles were now packed with mince pies, plum puddings, tins of shortbread and selection boxes. It wouldn't be long before the Christmas songs were once again filling the air waves. Imogen pushed her trolley along through the crowds, collecting up the ingredients she would need for dinner – chicken breasts, coconut milk, passata, sultanas, naan bread, rice … Just a few spices to flavour the sauce and she would be finished. She could see the little jars of chilli powder, turmeric, ginger and all the other things she required just a few feet away beyond the bottles of olive oil and balsamic vinegar but the area was thronging with people including two or three mothers chatting to each other whilst their children toddled alongside, pulling at their trolleys. Imogen just managed to edge her way through but then encountered several other obstacles blocking her path so, leaving her own trolley aside for a moment, she zigzagged her way around them to reach for the spice jars. Suddenly the ground just seemed to give way and she found herself flat on her back with one of the 'obstacles' clattering on top of her. With a jolt she realised what it was. A yellow 'slippery floor' sign.

As concerned shoppers hovered over her, offering to help her to her feet, Imogen just wished that the floor could swallow her up. She was sore all over and her clothes were smeared with cooking oil, but most of all she felt so stupid and embarrassed. It was perfectly obvious now why the aisle had been so cluttered. Four of the yellow signs had been hastily placed around the oil spillage while a member of staff went to fetch the necessary equipment to clean it up. Even as she lay there she could see a man approaching with a bucket and mop.

"I'll be OK in a minute," Imogen tried to reassure the crowd that had gathered around her as several worried voices reached her at once.

"Are you all right, Love?"

"Is there anyone I can call for you?"

"Do you think you've broken anything?"

"Shall I get the manager over?"

"Did you not see the sign?"

Imogen closed her eyes and willed them all to go away. Thank God there was no-one she knew to witness the commotion. It was bad enough that she had made a fool of herself in front of strangers. How could she not have noticed that those signs were there to warn her of the danger! She tried to stand up but just slipped again on the oil. The man with the bucket was now by her side and two other staff members had arrived in the aisle. Together they helped her to her feet. Then, ignoring her pleas of independence, the two kind ladies escorted Imogen to the manager's office, collecting her trolley of groceries on the way, whilst the young man began to clean up the mess and ensure the safety of other shoppers.

"I'm so sorry," Imogen began as soon as the manager came through the door, having been briefed about the incident by the two assistants. "This was entirely my own fault. I was walking about in a daze and didn't notice the warning signs. You don't need to worry; I won't be suing the store or anything."

"Grant Cartwright," the store manager replied, introducing himself and extending his right hand in her direction. "I just want to make sure that you're all right. I was told you took quite a fall."

Imogen accepted the handshake and looked up. "I'm just a bit shaken," she stammered. "I'm sure I've jarred a few muscles. I'll probably feel it more tomorrow." Suddenly she found herself quivering and wasn't sure whether it was some kind of delayed shock or a reaction to Mr Cartwright's kindness and good looks, the touch of his skin. He was still holding her hand and she liked it. One of the ladies who had helped her to her feet, arrived at the door with two coffees and some ginger nut biscuits.

"Thanks, Bronagh," said Mr Cartwright, letting go of Imogen's hand and taking hold of the tray. Bronagh smiled at Imogen and left them alone. "We should fill out an accident report form just in case," the manager then proposed. "It's store policy no matter what the circumstances." He proceeded to check her details and fill them in on the form while they drank their coffee. Imogen once more assured him that she was not blaming his staff for what had happened but she was happy to comply with the rules and gave him the requested information. She then insisted that she was feeling much better and would be able to drive herself home as planned. He accompanied her to her car after picking up the remaining items she needed and throwing in a complimentary box of chocolates. As he held the car door open for her, Imogen noticed that he was wearing a wedding ring. She found herself feeling disappointed and thinking that his wife was a very lucky woman. In fact Imogen felt quite jealous.

Back at the flat a warm bath filled with fragrant soapy bubbles was working wonders on her bruised muscles as Imogen tried to put the embarrassment of the afternoon behind her. She even began to see the funny side of it. How ridiculous she must have looked, wending her way between those yellow signs and deliberately walking through the danger zone without a care in the world. Well, it would make for an amusing anecdote for her supper guests. She might even mention the incident on her blog, as a precautionary tale for others. Jillian would be home soon and would probably suggest cancelling the proposed curry supper if she was aware of what had taken place. So she wouldn't tell her. Not yet anyway. With a fair degree of surprise, Imogen suddenly realised that she didn't actually feel any envy towards Jillian at all. She was welcome to Bradley Harrington. Instead her thoughts returned to that hand on her car door, that hand with the bright, shiny wedding band which had flashed in her eyes telling her that he was taken. The soft, sexy tone of his voice as he questioned her about her fall. The way he licked his lips when he was eating his biscuit and drinking his coffee. The warmth of his handshake and the tingling sensation that accompanied it. She felt it again now, lying in the bath with her eyes closed. There was an unmistakeable attraction. Imogen sighed with a modicum of self-pity. She wouldn't dream of starting a relationship with a married man. No matter how tempting. No matter what means of seduction he employed. Maybe he would turn out to have a twin brother!

★★★

Supper was a great success. Jillian and Bradley both complimented Imogen on her delicious curry and the conversation remained focused on general topics of interest so that there was no awkwardness between the two girls. Bradley noticed the stiffness of movement when Imogen finally rose from the table to take the plates into the kitchen.

"Are you OK?" he asked with some concern.

"Took a bit of a tumble earlier on," she now admitted. "I've jarred a few muscles."

"Why didn't you say?" Jillian admonished her. "We could have put this off for another day."

Imogen smiled and then started to laugh as she related the events of the afternoon. She soon had her friends giggling too as they visualised her squeezing into the sealed off area, carefully avoiding the yellow floor signs themselves whilst stepping directly onto the lethal patch of slime.

"So you did see the signs?" Jillian probed, looking for confirmation. "You knew what they were?"

"They were as plain as the nose on your face. I just wasn't thinking straight, didn't register what they were or why they would have been placed there. I just saw them as obstacles I had to get round! I must have looked like a real idiot."

Another round of laughter was interrupted by a phone ringing in the kitchen. "That'll be mine," Imogen said. "I've left it on charge in there." She hobbled out of the room to take the call, leaving Jillian and Bradley at the table.

"How about coffee upstairs?" Bradley suggested with a nod upwards towards his own flat. "Just you and me. Let Imogen have an early night."

Jillian's heart missed a beat. She wondered whether he really meant coffee or maybe something more. Only one way to find out. Nodding her head in agreement she insisted that they help clear the dishes away first but Imogen shooed them away, reading the situation quite accurately. She would be happy to have the place to herself and to nurse her wounds in peace. Her friends slipped out the door and up to Bradley's apartment.

Imogen's phone rang again. She hadn't answered it the first time, never did accept calls from unknown numbers. This time, however, something made her curious. She held it to her ear. "Hello?"

"Hi Imogen. It's Grant. Just wondering how you are."

"Grant?"

"Grant Cartwright. From the supermarket."

"Oh, Mr Cartwright! That's very nice of you to ring. I'm a bit sore but I'll survive. I still can't get over my stupidity."

"I hope it won't put you off shopping in our store."

"No, of course not. But I'll try to keep my wits about me in future."

"It would be nice to see you again. Make sure you call in at the office next time you're in. We can have coffee again and another chat."

Imogen felt a bit confused. "Why would you want me to do that?" she quizzed. "I already told you I accept full responsibility for what happened. Your staff had taken all reasonable precautions. There is nothing for you to worry about."

"I just thought it would be nice to see you again."

"Why?"

"Because I liked you. I'm sure I felt some chemistry between us."

"And your wife would be happy to know that?"

Silence. A deadly silence that seemed to go on for ever.

"Look," Imogen said at last, "I'm not denying that I felt an attraction too. But I noticed you were wearing a ring. And I don't date married men. Full stop."

"That's very commendable but …"

"Do you deny that you were wearing a wedding ring?"

"No, but …"

Imogen decided it was time to end this conversation. "On second thoughts," she declared, "I think I will do my shopping somewhere else from now on. Please don't ring me again. I appreciated your help this afternoon but I don't want to take things any further. Good-bye Mr Cartwright." Before he even had time to respond she disconnected the call and promptly burst into tears. Why did her relationships always have to be so complicated? And where was Jillian when she most needed her? Upstairs, snogging the bloody face off Bradley Harrington! Without further ado Imogen cleared away the rest of the supper dishes and went straight to bed. What a god-awful day it had been. A huge bruise had now appeared on her thigh and a smaller one on her elbow. Her whole body ached. Close to tears again she eased herself into a comfortable position and took a deep breath. And then she caught sight of her mother's diary on her bedside table.

I am no closer to solving that mystery. There is sure to be some commonplace explanation for what my mum has written there. I'll go round tomorrow and collect the 1990 book. Just to satisfy my curiosity. I'm sure it'll turn out to be nothing. So why don't I just ask her? No, it would be too embarrassing; she'd think I was prying. That's not really an option. I feel so alone tonight. I wonder what Sam is doing.

Once the thought entered her head there was no getting rid of it. She reached out for her phone and scrolled through the numbers in her contact list. She had never got round to deleting him. She gazed at his name now and she wanted him. More than ever. She longed to hear his voice. And before she realised what she was really doing, she had activated the call function. His phone was ringing.

"Hello?"

That same voice that she remembered so well. Those husky tones.

"Hello? Who's calling please?"

He didn't know who it was. So he hadn't kept her contact details. She had just come up as an unknown number.

Well why would he have kept my details? He's with Holly now.

Tears started to trickle down her cheeks anew.

"Is that you, Imogen?"

"Yes."

"Is something wrong? Why are you ringing me?"

"I just needed to hear your voice, to talk to you."

She heard a heavy sigh on the other end of the line. Then she was aware of a woman's voice in the background, a woman trying to entice him away from the phone.

"It's not a good time, Imogen."

"Sorry. At least let me talk to Holly. Please."

"Holly isn't here."

"But I just heard her."

"That wasn't Holly. I'm not with Holly anymore."

Imogen gasped in disbelief.

"But you left me for Holly."

"It didn't work out."

A myriad of thoughts flooded her brain.

Sam's free again and nobody told me. Maybe it's not too late. We were happy once. We could be happy again. But could I trust him? Would he do it again, find another Holly? Surely it's worth taking a chance.

The female voice in the background was now sounding impatient. Imogen felt peeved.

"I've had such a crap day, Sam. And now you're telling me that you don't want me, even though your fling with Holly is over."

"I have to go, Imogen."

"At least tell me why it didn't work out."

"Ask Holly. Goodnight Imogen. I'm sorry you haven't found happiness."

And the line went dead.

Imogen was completely riled up after this exchange and could not settle. She called Holly.

"I hear that you've split from Sam," she thundered accusingly at the girl who had ruined the only relationship she had ever valued. "What went wrong?"

Holly spoke with a calm resignation. "Hello Imogen. I just couldn't take it any longer."

"Couldn't take what?"

"The way he was always talking about you. Imogen this and Imogen that. I got sick of listening to it."

"But he doesn't want me!"

"I know. That's what makes it all so ridiculous. I told him he should go back to you but he said he couldn't live in the past. He said he couldn't expect you to take him back after what he had done. So he hooked up with Tania and now she's pregnant."

"She's what?"

"Pregnant. She's having his baby. It must be due soon."

When there was no response Holly softened her tone and told her erstwhile friend that she would keep her abreast of developments. "I never meant to hurt you and it wasn't even worth it in the end," she added. "He's turned out to be a total commitment phobe. You're better off without him. I actually feel sorry for Tania."

Exhausted, confused and angry, Imogen ended the call and closed her eyes, allowing herself to wallow in a moment of self-pity. Bradley had chosen Jillian over her. Sam had chosen Tania. And Grant Cartwright was married. But as she finally drifted into a deep, deep sleep, only one out of those three potential lovers continued to pull at her heartstrings.

Chapter 7

"Come on, you're the security expert. Surely you can find a way for me to get in." Jillian had not lifted her key when she had gone up to Bradley's flat for coffee and now she found herself locked out. Imogen had obviously fallen asleep.

"I don't want to break your lock," Bradley reasoned with her. "I'm not a magician. You can either hammer on the door until she hears you or you can come back upstairs with me."

"It's late. I want to go to bed."

"That can be arranged."

"Very funny. I want to go to *my* bed. There are things that I need."

"I might be able to supply them. Try me."

Jillian was not sure whether this was just idle banter or whether he really was suggesting that they sleep together. She didn't know what to do. Bradley took her hand and led her to the staircase. "Come and have another coffee for a start," he proposed, "or a glass of wine. Take half an hour and then give her a ring. The phone's sure to wake her up."

"I haven't even got my phone," she replied in exasperation. "I just walked out with you without lifting anything."

Bradley remained calm. "Don't worry," he reminded her, "I have her number in my phone."

They went back into his flat and he produced a glass of wine. Jillian took a sip and sank back into the luxurious brown leather with a sigh of resignation. "So tell me about Della," she relented. "Who dumped who?"

Bradley flinched. "I don't like the word 'dumped'," he told her. "It was kind of mutual. It just fizzled out."

"Sorry," Jillian pleaded, "I don't like that word either. I don't even know why I used it."

"Nerves?" Bradley suggested.

Jillian set down her wine glass and looked him straight in the eye. "Why should I be nervous?"

"Well, I am."

"Nervous about what?"

"You. It's very soon, I know. But you and me together here. Alone. And you locked out of your own place. It's as if this was meant to happen. But it's up to you. I won't do anything if you don't want me to." He knew he was rambling but there was no response so he just kept going. "I never loved Della. It was just a bit of fun. We're still on friendly terms if we bump into each other. But you're gorgeous, Jillian. I really do think I'm falling in love with you." Still no response. He hoped he hadn't put his foot in it and scared her off. "What about your own previous relationships? Has there been anyone special? Say something."

"I don't know what to say. We've only known each other for a matter of weeks. We don't really know each other at all." She knew she was saying the right words. But there was something gnawing at her, trying to make her say something else. "And no, there hasn't been anyone special in my life up to now."

"Don't you believe in love at first sight? My parents fell in love from the very first time they saw each other and they're still together today. Maybe it runs in the family."

"You think that you love me?"

"I think I do."

"And that makes you nervous?"

Bradley took her in his arms and kissed her. "Yes, I'm nervous that I'll spoil things between us by making a move too soon. But talk about a missed opportunity! Where *are* you going to sleep tonight?"

"I could drive home. My family home isn't far away."

"And where are your keys?"

"Ah!" A seductive smile accompanied the exclamation, telling Bradley that she was only teasing him. She had no intention of driving home. He decided to test her resolve.

"I'll call you a taxi," he said. "I can't take you myself since I've been drinking."

Jillian lifted her glass and drank the rest of her wine in one gulp as she searched her brain for a good answer but words evaded her. Instead she just shook her head and took Bradley by the hand. "Why don't you give me a guided tour," she whispered at last.

"Of my apartment or my body?" he replied, his eyes full of mischief.

"Both," breathed Jillian. "And be sure not to leave anything out. I want the full package."

"That will not be a problem," Bradley agreed, as he led her through to the bedroom. "The full package it is."

★★★

"No regrets?" The wintry light was filtering through the dove grey blinds into Bradley's bedroom, illuminating his face which was smiling at her with a mixture of naughtiness and content. Jillian reached out and gently touched it.

"What do you think?" she muttered dreamily, arching her body towards him yet again.

"Admit it," he teased, "you locked yourself out last night on purpose."

"I did nothing of the sort," Jillian protested quite vehemently, edging away from him again.

"I'm only joking." His eyes were dancing as he pulled her back into an embrace and kissed her on the lips. She kissed him back. The bed was warm and cosy, the smell of sex lingering on the sheets mingled with his manly scent and her own spicy perfume. It was intoxicating and they were both naked under the black and white striped duvet. There was only one thing to do…

★★★

Hobbling to answer the door in her blue, fleecy robe, Imogen was confused to find her friend still wearing the red dress she had sported last night for dinner. Definitely not her normal attire for a Sunday morning. And what was she doing out so early anyway? And her hair was a bit dishevelled. No handbag. But a rosy glow to her cheeks. The penny dropped.

"You never even missed me," Jillian chided her.

"I'm only just up. I thought you were still asleep."

"I didn't have my key. Or anything else."

"But you obviously managed to find a bed for the night."

Jillian just smiled and nodded, confirming her friend's assumption. Then she realised that Imogen was limping quite badly. "Let me take a shower and then I'll do us some breakfast," she said kindly. "You should take it easy for today."

"I've really stiffened up from that fall yesterday," Imogen replied, displaying the large bruise on her leg. "But I want to call with Mum and Dad later to pick up another diary. Mum's ramblings are quite fascinating."

"I'll come with you if you like," Jillian offered. "It would save you having to drive."

Imogen was happy to accept both the breakfast and the lift to her parents' house. She hobbled back to her room and lay down again while Jillian got washed and changed. She had not yet confided in her flat-mate but she really needed to talk to someone about that weird entry in her mother's diary. What could it mean? She picked up the book and had another look. It just didn't add up. But some sixth sense told her that something significant had taken place on 10th November 1990, something really significant. And she wouldn't be able to relax until she got to the bottom of it.

They were both enjoying their coffee and pancakes when a knock at the door heralded another visit from Bradley.

"We're all invited to a party next Saturday," he announced. "Alastair's cousin is twenty-one next week and they're having a big celebration. I hope you can both come. The more the merrier."

"We don't even know him," said Imogen, "let alone his cousin!"

"But you'll be my guests," Bradley insisted. "Granny Gertrude is organising it. You will absolutely love her. She has been so supportive to me over the years. She's a fabulous person. Please come. You won't regret it."

"Granny Gertrude?"

"She's Alastair's granny. But she has been like another granny to me. Ever since Alastair and I became buddies at school. There's nothing she likes more than a big party. Any excuse! But twenty-one? That's a pretty good reason for a celebration."

"But why is she including us in the invitation?"

Bradley put his arm round Jillian. "I told her that I couldn't come without my new girlfriend and her lovely flat-mate," he pronounced. "So you'll both come?"

"Why not?" Jillian quirked, relishing the touch of his skin so soon after their love-making.

"It's nice of you to include me," added Imogen. "Thanks."

"What should we bring for a present?" asked Jillian. "Is this cousin male or female?"

"It's a girl. Rebecca. Just bring a bottle of wine or something. Or chocolates. No need for anything fancy. I'll book a taxi for the three of us. Seven o'clock OK?"

"Perfect. We'll look forward to it."

And he was gone. It was nice to have something to prepare for. And it was lovely that he had included the both of them.

Later in the day Jillian drove Imogen over to her parents' house. She listened patiently as, once again, Imogen explained what had happened to her in the supermarket. Only this time Imogen wasn't so magnanimous about the way she had been treated by the store manager. In fact she was quite scathing about his behaviour. Jillian just put it down to the pain and discomfort that her friend was suffering. She knew nothing about the phone-call that had annoyed her so much.

"Anyway," Imogen came to the main point of the visit, "I am returning your 1991 diary." She took it from her bag and handed it over. "I'd love to see another one. Maybe something from in between the two I've read. When I was about two or three." Fingers crossed. She didn't want to give herself away by being too specific. But in truth she was only interested in the 1990 one now. She had to know what had happened on 10th November of that year. She had confided in Jillian on the way over, showing her the entry that had intrigued her and she too had found it fascinating but had also been cautious, warning her friend that there may have

59

been things that happened in the past that would best be forgotten. Imogen had assured her that she would not mention it to her mother; she just wanted to satisfy her own curiosity.

Joanna left the room and the girls chatted for some minutes to Keith, telling him about their new friend and the forthcoming party at Gertrude's house. He talked about how things were going at work and how he was looking forward to his imminent retirement and the plans he and Joanna had been making. They were hoping to do a lot of travelling around the globe while they were still in good health and young enough to enjoy it. Imogen couldn't relax. Her thoughts fluctuated between last night's ill-advised conversations with Sam and Holly and the phone call from the married store manager along with her concerns about the diary issue. Several minutes passed.

Following her mum upstairs when she still hadn't returned, accompanied by Toby who was yelping with excitement at having her back home, Imogen discovered Joanna sitting on the bed leafing through some of her memoirs herself. The wardrobe door was wide open and for a moment Joanna appeared to be annoyed that Imogen had intruded into her private space. Other books could clearly be seen at the back of the bottom shelf and it was quite obvious that they would normally be hidden by the pile of jumpers now sitting on the floor. Imogen pretended that she hadn't noticed, that she was just playing chasies with the dog. Joanna handed her the two books she was holding and hurriedly ushered her out of the room. Imogen glanced at the front covers and frowned. 1989 and 1993. Well, at least she knew where to look on another occasion. She realised at once that it was a disingenuous thought. But she just couldn't help herself.

Chapter 8

"You should take a few days off," Jillian advised her friend as she turned off the television on Sunday evening. "And if I were you, I'd be putting a claim in against that store. Just because they put warning signs up doesn't mean they weren't negligent. They were too slow reacting to the danger."

"I'd love to take that smug look off the manager's face," Imogen replied, "but it really was my own fault. Just let it be."

Jillian was confused. "I thought you said the manager was nice," she said.

"He was. Very nice."

"So what has changed all of a sudden?"

"He phoned me up last night."

"You exchanged phone numbers? You never told me that, you dark horse."

Imogen sighed. "He had my number from the injury report form."

"Oh, so he was just checking up on how you were. What's wrong with that?"

"He was coming on to me. And he's married. The sleaze ball."

"Married? Don't touch him with a barge pole," Jillian agreed. "I'll tell him where to go if he comes sniffing around here."

"You could do an article on him for your magazine," Imogen said in jest knowing that Jillian's professionalism wouldn't allow it. "Expose him for what he is. The thing is, I really did like him yesterday and actually felt quite jealous of his wife but I feel sorry for her now. I wonder whether she knows what he's like. I'm sure it's not the first time he has tried it on with someone else." She paused for a moment and then decided to confide in her friend concerning the other phone calls she had made. "I was in such a bad mood afterwards that I did something really stupid."

Jillian raised her eyebrows. "What did you do?" she asked.

"I phoned Sam."

"Sam!"

"I know. You don't need to say it. I told you it was stupid."

Jillian spoke in a voice that depicted both exasperation and empathy. "Oh, Imogen, you shouldn't have. Sam was nearly two years ago. You're surely not still holding a torch for him."

"I still miss him."

"He's with Holly."

"He's not. They've split."

Jillian looked at her wide-eyed. "You're not thinking

of taking him back? He'll do it again, Imogen. He'll break your heart all over again."

"He's with somebody called Tania. She's pregnant."

"Well there you are!" exclaimed Jillian. "You sure know how to pick them."

"It was just a spur of the moment thing," Imogen assured her. "I won't do it again. I've definitely got him out of my system now."

Jillian hoped that was true. She tried to change the subject. "I'm really enjoying the research for this month's edition of the magazine," she now revealed. "It's all about people who run evening classes for adults. I'm very tempted to join up for some of the courses myself."

"I've often thought about doing an art class," Imogen agreed. "Or pottery."

Jillian remarked that she was considering one on creative writing, adding that she had been inspired by a young woman called Maggie whom she had recently interviewed for the upcoming edition. As well as the particular course she was considering she added that Maggie also takes a more basic one on adult literacy skills, mainly aimed at people who have left school without a decent standard of reading and spelling.

"Gosh, that sounds a bit boring," Imogen scoffed.

"Actually, it's quite fascinating," Jillian countered. "For example, how do you spell **e**?"

"What do you mean? There's no such word."

"It's not a word. It's a sound. How do you spell the sound **e**?" She pronounced it like the sound of the letter name when reciting the alphabet.

"With the letter 'e' doubled up," Imogen suggested. "Like in the word 'bee'. I was stung by a bee." Jillian's tactic had worked nicely, putting her aches and pains along with her cheating store manager and former boyfriend right out of her mind.

"That's right," Jillian agreed. "But what about a single 'e' as in 'he' or 'she' or 'me'? It makes the same sound."

"I suppose it does. I never really thought about it."

"And then there's 'ea' as in 'tea' or 'flea'."

"OK."

"And 'ie' as in 'niece'."

"I before e except after c," put in Imogen.

"Exactly! That's another one, 'ei' as in 'ceiling'."

"So that makes five ways of spelling the same sound. No wonder so many people get confused."

"There are more than five," Jillian blustered, becoming quite animated. "Think about it. There's 'y' as in 'happy' and 'ey' as in donkey. Maggie could give you an even longer list. I can't remember them all now."

"But it's just the **e** sound that causes all the problems? The other letters are normal aren't they?"

"Well, you tell me. How do you spell **o**?"

"'Oh'. Or just 'o' like in 'solo'. That's two, right enough."

"Keep thinking."

"'So', 'go', 'hello', 'open'. It's always just the one letter. Apart from the exclamation, 'oh'."

"What about 'boat' and 'goat'? That's 'oa'."

"So it is. Didn't think of that."

"And then there's 'oe' as in 'toe' or 'potatoes' and 'ough' as in 'though'."

"Ah!"

"And 'ow' as in 'arrow' or 'borrow' or 'own'."

"Got you! That's where your theory falls down. 'Ow' doesn't always sound like that. What about 'owl' or 'now' or 'bow' as in 'bow down' as opposed to 'ribbons and bows'. And what about 'bough' for that matter, as in the branch of a tree?"

"I never said it did make sense! That's just a further complication. I'm telling you, it's fascinating. I could have listened to Maggie for hours."

Imogen decided she could take no more for now. "I'm off to bed to read these diaries," she said, bringing the conversation to a close. "I'll let you know if I find anything interesting."

The diaries had really failed to stimulate any further interest for her now so she read a few chapters of her novel first. But that one entry kept coming to mind. What could it mean? Nothing else seemed to matter. She lifted the 1993 book first and turned straight to the allotted date. Holding her breath she read what Joanna had written.

Three years on. We never talk about it. Still feel so guilty but have to forget it ever happened. We have covered our tracks and no-one will ever know. But that little boy - I just wish I knew, one way or the other.

What the hell does that mean? Imogen was distraught. She just had to find out what this was all about. She struggled out of bed and made her way to Jillian's room but was met with total silence. Her friend was already asleep. She returned to her own room and started leafing through the rest of the book. A bomb had killed two children in Warrington. Imogen remembered reading about that incident. It had obviously had an emotional impact on Joanna when she had mentioned it in her diary. How awful that two young lives had been snuffed out in such horrendous circumstances. Life can be so unfair. She turned a few more pages. Pete Sampras and Steffi Graff had been the Wimbledon champions. A couple of recipes had been copied in. More visits to the doctor. Christmas parties. Normal activities for a mother and her six-year-old daughter. Nothing to help her solve the mystery. She set the book down and opened the other one. 1989. A disaster at Hillsborough Football Stadium in Sheffield. Imogen had certainly heard about that event. Sure it had been on the news recently with the inquest still ongoing all these years later. But her mother's diaries were making it all so real. What a dreadful thing to have happened. All those lives lost at what should have been a normal day watching football. Yet another win for Steffi Graff with Boris Becker taking the men's Wimbledon title this time. A night out at the cinema with Keith for *Shindler's List* and another for *Sleepless in Seattle*. Imogen had seen both films for herself. Both brilliant. It was nice to think of her parents viewing them as new releases. But it didn't help her solve the mystery. What happened on 10th November 1990? Imogen closed the book and went back to her novel.

Chapter 9

"Miss Redpath, please. The governors are ready for you now."

Maggie stood up and followed the suited gentleman into the Board Room where six people were seated around three sides of a large square table. She sat down on the lone chair at the front of the room, as directed. The gentleman then introduced himself and the other governors and tried to put her at ease, explaining that there would be four main questions to answer followed by an opportunity for her to make any further comments which might enhance her application for the post. She would have approximately twenty-five minutes in total. He added that they were interviewing seven people altogether and that the school principal would telephone the successful candidate the following morning. Maggie smiled and nodded, confirming that she understood the arrangements and took a sip from the glass of water which had been placed on a little table to her right.

The Chairman asked the first question himself.

Would you please outline your career to date and give us an indication of any particular qualifications, experience or aptitudes which you can bring to this post? Thank you.

Good. She had been hoping for a general starter question, one where she could just talk about her achievements and the things that interest her in life. She remembered the advice she had been given by her uncle.

Don't assume that all the governors have read your application form or that any of them will remember anything you wrote on it. The purpose of the form is simply to ensure that you meet the criteria for the job. Obviously you do or you wouldn't have got to this stage. But you have to be aware that the same is true for everyone else who has been selected for interview. So the form is no longer relevant. The interview panel will only take into account anything that you actually mention in person on the day.

Thank goodness she had an uncle who knew the system and indeed an uncle who took such an interest in her life. She certainly couldn't rely on her father. Maggie launched into the answer she had prepared, making sure that she talked about her degree modules and all the other courses she had attended since graduating as well as the literacy classes she was now taking herself. She outlined the experience she had gathered working as a substitute teacher and tried to give the panel some insight into her personality and wider interests. She had done her homework, reading up about the school and its policies and she felt sure that she could fit in and make a difference to the lives of these particular children. Hopefully she was getting that message across. She watched the seven governors taking copious notes as she spoke. They must be writing down almost everything she said, word for word. But was she impressing them? There was no way of knowing. Their expressions remained impassive throughout. When Maggie stopped speaking, they simply moved on to a new page and prepared to start all over again. No-one asked her to clarify anything or made any comment on what she had said. A woman who had been introduced as a parent governor asked the second question.

The school has a very strong anti-bullying policy. Can you explain how you would approach a parent who came to you complaining that a child in your class was being bullied?

Maggie took a deep breath and then had another sip of water while she gathered her thoughts. Nerves had made her throat seem quite dry. Then she faced the panel again, all sitting with their pencils poised, ready to scribble down her words of wisdom. She had to come up with a better answer than those other six people. Well, she would do her best.

"If I am successful in this application," she then began, "the first thing I will do is gather up the school's policies and read them, especially the key ones such as pastoral care, safeguarding, discipline and anti-bullying." She paused and looked around her. Several heads were nodding in agreement. Good. "There are bullies in every school," she continued, "but there are also people who use the term loosely to describe any type of aggressive behaviour without really understanding the meaning of the word." Maggie paused again, realising that it was important to answer the exact question she had been asked and not to go off at a tangent. She asked the lady to repeat the question and then continued.

"I would thank the parent concerned for bringing this to my attention and would assure him or her that it would be fully investigated as a matter of urgency. What I would do next would depend on what is in the policy. All schools are slightly different in their approach to such things. I know this from my experience of subbing. But I think it is important that, within a school, there needs to be a joined-up approach with everyone following the same rules."

Maggie looked around the room again. Seven pairs of eyes were looking at her, seven pencils poised waiting for more.

"Children who engage in bullying behaviour often need help themselves, just as much as the victim."

A couple of heads nodded in agreement.

"But I think it is imperative that an important policy like anti-bullying is always under review. When I say that everyone should follow the same rules, I am not implying that I would never question those rules. There has to be room for change, for improvement, for fresh ideas. But schools have a hierarchy of authority and that has to be respected. So, if I had an idea of something that might work in a particular situation, I would bring it to the principal or the appropriate co-ordinator for discussion. In the short term my main focus would be careful observation of the child or children concerned to make sure they are happy and safe."

Maggie realised that she hadn't given a detailed list of the actions she would expect to carry out but she hoped she had said enough. She waited for the third question. It came from an elderly man with thinning grey hair and gold-rimmed spectacles.

Can you please tell us your views on the value of homework in the changing society that we live in nowadays?

Gosh, she hadn't thought of that one, had no answer prepared. She wasn't even sure whether the school had a homework policy or not. She would just have to speak from the heart.

"I think the crux of the matter," she began, "is in the phrase 'changing society that we live in nowadays'. In many ways education is still functioning in the past. It is assumed that children are going home after their day at school to eat a meal at the family table and then settle down with mother while father relaxes after a hard day's work. This is in so many ways a very antiquated perception of how families operate in the modern world."

She paused and looked around for some clue that she was on the right track but there was nothing. They were all sitting with their pencils poised for her next remark.

"Homework has traditionally been the responsibility

of the mother, at primary level anyway. But let's be realistic. Many children today do not have the luxury of living with both parents. For many the reality is that there is only one parent, usually the mother, and that she is likely to be exhausted after a day's work followed by the task of making a meal and carrying out all the other routine household chores. The last thing she needs is an extension of her child's day at school, or more often than not, her children's experience at school. When you consider that she might have four or five children all at different stages of the curriculum and maybe a baby or toddler as well, there is every chance of the evening turning into a total nightmare of onerous toil and stress."

When she looked around this time some of the panel members were looking decidedly interested.

"Then we have to consider the growing number of children who live in two separate homes, spending part of the week with one parent and part of it with the other. The two adults might approach the topic of homework in completely different ways so that the children become confused or frustrated. The thing that concerns me most is that some teachers do not understand these issues and are too quick to blame the child who comes to school without the set work being completed."

Maggie was not at all sure that she was saying what the governors wanted to hear. Nevertheless she was well into her stride now and to some extent speaking from experience. She decided to keep going.

"I have come across various homework policies in the schools where I have subbed," she now revealed. "In one school I was in recently the first session of the morning was spent going over the work that had been done at home with the children reading out their answers and marking their own books or in some cases checking each other's work. There is definitely a lot of merit in this approach because the explanations are provided as you go along and there is an opportunity to ask questions rather than just receive a list of ticks and crosses at the end of the day. However, a vast amount of time was wasted trying to ascertain who had not completed the work and whether there was an acceptable reason for the omission. I came across various scenarios whereby the missing work had to be completed during a lunch-break or while the other children were engaging in some kind of fun activity. In some cases they were simply told to do a double homework the following night. I can understand that those who conform and regularly do the set work would take umbrage if their peers were simply allowed to get away with it but I have to say I have concluded that it is not worth the time or the hassle or the falling out with parents. If I were in charge of a school I would do away with the concept of compulsory homework and would replace it with general advice to parents about ways that they can help their children at home."

Maggie suddenly realised that she might have gone too far. She smiled and concluded her answer by moderating her comments.

"But of course this current post would not put me

in charge of the school and, if I'm successful, I would follow whatever policy is in place in this as in all other matters."

There was one further question which dealt with Maggie's willingness to help out with extra-curricular activities and a chance to ask questions of her own, which she declined. She felt that she had said everything she wanted to. Hopefully she had managed to impress the panel.

Chapter 10

By Saturday Imogen was feeling quite well again and looking forward to the night out with Jillian and Bradley. The three of them had clubbed together and bought a nice necklace for the party girl. After all, turning twenty-one was a big event, even if the two girls didn't actually know Rebecca. Bradley assured them he didn't really know her very well himself. But he was very fond of Gertrude. In her early seventies now, she was apparently quite a character and had taken Bradley under her wing when, as a child, he had befriended her grandson. Over the years she had loved organising parties where Alastair could be integrated with a wider population and not just those few friends he had from his own special school. Bradley was convinced that Alastair's physical and even more so his mental development had been given a huge boost thanks to her concerted efforts in making his life as normal as possible. Imogen and Jillian were both proud to be associated with someone who was in turn associated with such a delightful family. They were looking forward to meeting them all.

Emerging from the taxi at seven-thirty, both girls gazed open-mouthed at the luxurious surroundings.

"You didn't tell us she lived in a mansion," Jillian quipped.

Bradley paid the driver and then led them up the tree-lined driveway which was currently covered in crisp autumn leaves. "It's not a mansion," he laughed, "but it does have a lovely big garden. You should see it when the daffodils and tulips are out in the springtime. It's gorgeous."

"So this is where Alastair developed his interest in gardening," put in Imogen. "Didn't you tell us he works in a garden centre?"

"That's right," Bradley nodded as they reached the house and found that it wasn't a mansion right enough, more like a quaint country cottage. There was a Christmas tree illuminated with twinkling coloured lights in front of the large bay window, reminding them all that it was only three days away from December. As they walked past the three cars that were parked side by side and up to the front door, the merry sound of music could be heard from inside. Bradley rang the bell.

From the moment they entered the house, it was clear to both girls that these were decent and friendly people who knew how to enjoy themselves. Gertrude welcomed them all with open arms as Bradley introduced Jillian as his girlfriend and Imogen as her best friend. Gertrude was flamboyant in a bright red and orange tunic which she wore loosely over comfortable-looking burgundy trousers. A jangly necklace of big orange and yellow beads and matching dangling earrings along with several colourful bracelets completed her outfit. She looked like the epitome of eccentricity.

"Come and meet Rebecca and her friends," Gertrude said, leading them straight into the kitchen where a bevy of glamorous girls and a few young men were chatting in animated voices. Jillian handed over the gift they had brought and everyone admired the piece of jewellery as the birthday girl tried it on. Escorted into the sitting-room next, the girls were introduced to Rebecca's mother, Catherine, and Gertrude's other daughter, Thomasina, both of whom greeted Bradley with warm affection. He was obviously held in high regard in this family. There were also two young men in the room over by the Christmas tree at the window. Jillian immediately recognised one of them to be Alastair but Imogen was now staring open-mouthed at the other one. She couldn't believe it. It was Grant Cartwright.

Oblivious to the flash of recognition between Imogen and Grant, Bradley proceeded to introduce his guests to his friend, Alastair and Alastair's cousin, Grant. Imogen shook their hands politely. She was feeling very uncomfortable with this development but she could not make a scene amongst these lovely people. Now that she was face to face with him again, the strong attraction she had initially felt returned with a vengeance but was coupled with the abhorrence she had experienced after his phone-call. And she couldn't help wondering which one of those glamorous ladies in the kitchen was married to him. How should she react when introduced properly to the girl? Say nothing or dump him in it! Suddenly he was speaking to her.

"Hello, Imogen. This is an unexpected surprise. How lovely to see you again so soon."

Bradley and Jillian both looked at her with some bewilderment, expecting her to explain how she knew Rebecca's brother but she just nodded and managed a smile. She couldn't wait to get away from him. And yet, at the same time she liked the way he had spoken to her, the way he looked at her. This was torture. Bradley started a conversation with Alastair and the two girls made their way back to the kitchen where they were offered a drink. Rebecca poured them both a glass of wine.

"So how do you know the cousin?" Jillian whispered as she took a sip of her wine.

"You'll never believe it." she told her friend. "He's the guy from the supermarket."

"The married bloke who was coming on to you? Wow! He *is* pretty dishy."

Imogen took another look at the faces around her. Maybe that tall blonde girl in the corner. Or the one with the dark curls and flawless complexion. She didn't know whether to feel sorry for the wife or jealous of her. She decided to ask anyway and take it from there. "So which one of you is married to Grant?" she asked in a cheerful voice, downing a gulp of her Merlot.

Everyone stopped talking at once and gazed in her direction. It just happened to be during a break in the music. You could have heard a pin drop.

"None of us is married to Grant," the beautiful dark-haired girl answered at last. "Zoe isn't here."

A subdued murmur of conversation started up again but no-one said anything else on the subject of Rebecca's brother and his wife. One girl, who looked younger than the rest, kept her eyes firmly on Imogen's face making her feel very awkward. Imogen edged away from the group, out into the hallway. Jillian followed her.

"That was a bit weird," Jillian remarked.

"At least I know her name. Zoe. She's obviously not welcome at family parties."

Suddenly Imogen felt a presence behind her and glanced over her shoulder. The younger girl had followed them out of the kitchen and had obviously overheard that last remark. "Hi," she said. "I'm Rebecca and Grant's other sister, Robyn. You've got it wrong. It's not that Zoe isn't welcome here."

"So Grant just doesn't bother to invite her? Somehow that doesn't surprise me."

"You don't seem to like him much."

"I don't really know him. But I don't have a lot of respect for married men who go chasing around after other women."

"He doesn't do that."

"Oh, yes he does."

Imogen took a deep breath, reminding herself that she was a guest in this house. And these were nice people. "Sorry," she apologised. "That just slipped out. It's none of my business. I hardly even know your brother."

Robyn touched her gently on the arm. "Zoe's dead,"

she whispered in a broken voice, unshed tears shining in her eyes. "She's dead. I just thought you should know." Then she turned on her heel and headed down the corridor which presumably led to the bedrooms. She opened a door and disappeared inside.

Imogen and Jillian stood stock still, trying to take in what they had just learnt. Imogen felt terrible. How could she have misread the situation so drastically wrong? What must those people in the kitchen be thinking about her? She felt sick. "I've got to get out of here," she mumbled. "I'm sorry, Jillian. I've really messed up. I'll call a taxi. You stay and enjoy the party. But I can't. I feel like such an idiot. But he was wearing a ring. How was I to know? Oh, God, what a nightmare. Dead!"

Jillian felt for her friend. She beckoned to Bradley who had just emerged from the sitting-room, looking for her. Quickly she explained what had just transpired. Bradley looked embarrassed. "I don't know Grant that well," he told her, "but I did know about his wife dying. I would have mentioned it if I had realised that either of you knew him but, well you must admit it's a bit of a coincidence. I had no idea. I'm sorry."

Grant was now standing by Bradley's elbow, smiling at the two girls. "I'm glad to see you have recovered from your fall, Imogen," he observed. "It really is a lovely surprise to ..." He stopped, picking up on the atmosphere. "What's wrong?" Bradley whispered something in his ear. He paled visibly. There was an awkward silence punctuated only by the background music which suddenly seemed so inappropriate. Bradley took Jillian's hand and gently led her away, back to the sitting-room where he could introduce her properly to Alastair. He had figured that Grant and Imogen would appreciate a bit of privacy. They would have things to discuss.

"Why didn't you tell me?" Imogen blurted out without thinking. "You've made a real fool out of me."

Grant flinched at her words. "I'm sorry," he faltered. "It's just not something I can talk about easily. I wanted to tell you, that night on the phone… but the words just wouldn't come."

Imogen pulled herself together. She wasn't the victim here. What right did she have to reprimand a grieving man? "I'm so sorry, Grant," she now avowed. "You have nothing to apologise for. I just got the wrong end of the stick. You still wear a wedding ring and I …"

"Can we go somewhere more private?" he proposed, stopping her in her tracks. "I'd like to tell you what happened."

Imogen just nodded. Grant took her by the hand and led her through the kitchen and out of the back door. She averted her gaze and tried to ignore the stares from the girls who had heard her ask her ham-fisted and gauche question a few minutes earlier. Grant picked up a key which was hanging by a hook near the door. Shivering in their party clothes, they walked down the garden path which was illuminated by security sensors as they passed by. Grant knew his granny's garden by heart and he knew that they wouldn't be disturbed in the summerhouse. He unlocked the door and led Imogen inside. It was freezing.

"It will be cosy in no time," Grant assured her, as

he plugged in the electric heater and lit some candles. He opened a trunk at the far end and took out a fluffy blanket. "Here, this will stop you shivering until the heat sets in."

Imogen surveyed her surroundings. It was the most fabulous garden retreat that she could imagine. They were totally alone, yet just down the path from the main house where the party was in full swing. She felt completely safe. But she didn't know what to say. And neither did he. They just sat side by side on the cane settee with the big, plump, green and pink cushions, each lost in their own thoughts. Grant was right about the efficient heating system. Even though it was late November, there was soon a pleasant warmth filling the air around them. But they kept the blanket anyway, for extra comfort.

"Tell me about Zoe," Imogen said at last.

"She was lovely," Grant reminisced dreamily. "She was beautiful and kind and generous."

Imogen gulped. "What happened to her?" she asked. "Was it some kind of accident?"

"No, she was ill," Grant revealed in a low and hesitant voice. "We knew she was terminally ill before the wedding. We brought it forward on purpose."

"Oh no!" breathed Imogen, the feeling of wretchedness that stemmed from her hostility towards this man over the past week pulling at her heartstrings and her conscience as the truth of the situation sank in. "I'm so, so sorry." She started to cry.

"It must be fate that you turned up here tonight," Grant now hinted. "I've been thinking about you all week, annoyed with myself for not telling you, for letting you think I was some kind of love rat. But I couldn't say it over the phone, I just couldn't."

"Of course not; I understand." She wiped the tears from her cheeks.

"We were only married for a few months. It was three years ago."

Imogen tried to smile. "It's lovely that you still wear your ring," she said in praise of his courage.

Grant sighed. "There just hasn't been the right moment to take it off. But I will. Soon." He cleared his throat. "Zoe made me promise to get on with my life, to make sure I didn't stay sad for too long. She was very brave." Tears came to his own eyes as he allowed that impassioned conversation to slip back into his conscious mind and he remembered just how brave his young bride had been. The endless hospital visits, the medication, the pain. Then he added, "I'm not surprised it was Robyn who told you. She was only thirteen at the time. It affected her badly."

"I'm so glad that she did before I made yet another faux pas. All those other people in the kitchen just looked at me in horror when I asked which one of them was married to you."

"So I wasn't wrong when I thought there was an attraction between us last Saturday?"

"No," Imogen admitted. "I felt it too." She paused. "Then your ring caught my eye as I was getting into the car."

Grant took her hand and smiled. "I'm going to keep

that promise I made to Zoe. I'll never forget her but I think I'm ready to move on. I hope you'll reconsider going out with me some evening. Now that you know the truth."

"You hadn't actually asked me out."

"I am now."

"Have you got a photo you could show me?"

He took out his phone and scrolled through his memories, selecting one of Zoe sitting on a boulder beside a fast-flowing river. Imogen recognised the surroundings at once. "Tollymore Park?" she asked him.

"Yes, that's right."

"She was beautiful."

"I know. And so are you."

"I'm not sure that I can compete with a ghost," Imogen said, unsure how to react to the evening's revelations.

"You don't need to worry about that," Grant assured her. "I promise you I will not make comparisons."

"But part of your heart will always belong to her." Imogen immediately realised that her remark sounded surly and petulant. She hadn't intended it to. Inwardly she rebuked herself and then added, "Which is only right and proper."

"I have a big heart. Try me."

She already had her mind made up. "OK."

Instinctively they embraced and it felt good. Then they kissed. It was tender and loving and they both let it linger, not wanting the kiss to end. It was another thirty minutes before they returned to Rebecca's party.

Chapter 11

Grant drove them all home. It turned out that his car was one of the three they had seen parked at the top of the driveway, a white Mazda. When he had heard Bradley say that he was about to phone for a taxi, Grant had insisted that it was no trouble. Imogen had watched, bemused, as he first went over to Catherine and confirmed that she and Robyn were staying over at Gertrude's place as planned and wouldn't need a lift themselves. There was some kind of exchange, probably keys she posited, and a very affectionate hug from both his mother and his sister. Imogen found that very touching; men didn't often hug their relatives in public in her experience. But then it had been a very emotional evening for Grant and she assumed that his behaviour was possibly out of the ordinary on that account.

Jillian suggested that the two men come in for coffee. They were now sitting in the girls' apartment chatting about cars whilst Jillian and Imogen busied themselves in the kitchen.

"That was a turn-up for the books," Jillian remarked

as she turned on the kettle. "I still can't get over it, your knight in shining armour turning up like that and not being the proverbial sleaze-ball after all."

"What do you think of him?" Imogen asked her dreamily.

"I like him. I think. Maybe a bit of a mummy's boy though. Need to be careful there." She too had noticed the exchange with his family just before they left the party.

Imogen put some instant coffee into the four mugs and reached for a packet of caramel wafers. She counted out four and set them on a tray, then poured some milk into a jug. They waited for the kettle to boil, each lost in their own thoughts about the evening. "Anyone take sugar?" she then called out as Jillian poured the water into the mugs.

"Two please," answered one voice.

"No, thanks," came the other reply.

The girls joined their guests in the lounge, Jillian beside Bradley on the burgundy sofa and Imogen on the wooden chair beside the coffee table where she set down the tray. She handed round the steaming mugs.

"So you two have known each other for years," Jillian said, addressing the two men.

"Sort of," Bradley confirmed. "We've met a few times at various events but never really got to know each other very well."

"Granny Gertrude and Aunt Thomasina just love Bradley," Grant put in. "To tell you the truth I used to be a bit jealous of him. They saw him as a real hero. I was just the cousin."

"Thanks for that!" rejoined Bradley with a grimace. He wasn't really offended, understood that it had been said at least partly in jest. Grant, on the other hand, was having a flashback to the time he had lost out on a football medal because Bradley had insisted on Alastair joining the team when another player hadn't turned up for the match. They had only been about twelve at the time and the tournament had been a relatively unimportant event organised by a local summer scheme but Grant had been fiercely competitive in all the sports he played and he had been furious when his cousin missed what would have been an easy goal for most other players. Alastair's delight in being included had turned to tears when several of the boys criticised and mocked him. Grant had just walked away, not actually joining in the slating but quietly seething with rage at the team's defeat. Only Bradley had stuck up for his friend. Grant remembered feeling really angry that night. But who was he angry with? Alastair, for losing them the game? Bradley, for picking him to play? The other boys, for their bullying tactics? His grandmother, for taking the three of them out for tea and making such a fuss of Bradley? All of those. But most of all he had been angry with himself and a bit ashamed. He pushed the memory from his mind.

"Are there no men on the scene? No fathers, uncles, grandfather?" It was Jillian who asked the question but both girls were thinking it.

"No," Grant replied. "My grandfather died about six years ago. He was a real gentleman. Alastair and I had great fun with him when we were little and then Rebecca and Robyn came along. They both worshipped him. He just took a heart attack one day and we never saw him again."

"Your granny copes pretty well on her own."

"She bounced back eventually. She's the one who holds our family together."

"So no fathers?"

"Well," Grant sighed, "Alastair's father is dead. Aunt Thomasina has never remarried and I don't think she ever will. She has never really managed to get over what happened. Alastair was a perfectly normal little boy before that accident and very intelligent. Now he lives quite a simple life compared to what it could have been. He spent about six weeks in hospital, getting home the day before Christmas Eve. He's always loved Christmas because of that. They're always the first people I know to get their Christmas tree up."

"Even though the accident had killed his father?"

"Thankfully he doesn't associate the two. He had already realised that his dad was gone, long before he got out of hospital."

"And what about your own dad? Is he still around?"

"Good question. I don't know."

"Oh." Jillian felt a bit awkward and apologised for asking.

"I love my mum," Grant now avowed, "but she's not great with relationships. With men I mean. She was never married to my dad and I never knew him."

"Oh, gosh, sorry," Jillian muttered, embarrassed. "This is none of my business."

"But you have two sisters," Imogen said, a confused look on her face.

"Half-sisters," Grant corrected her. "We have three different fathers. At least she does still see Robyn's father from time to time."

"But not Rebecca's?"

"No."

"That would seem so strange to me," Imogen commented. "I know it nearly seems old-fashioned in today's world but my parents have been together for ever, and Jillian's parents too. We're very ordinary."

Jillian nodded her head in agreement.

"Same goes for me," put in Bradley.

"I think that Mum is afraid to commit to anyone," Grant observed. "First Uncle Raymond died, then Grandfather. She saw how upset Thomasina and Gertrude were, how they struggled to cope, and she just decided not to put herself in a position where it could happen to her."

"That is so sad," Jillian sighed.

"She already had me before it all happened but I definitely think it stopped her forming a lasting relationship with the girls' fathers. That was Zoe's theory anyway."

At the mention of his wife's name, the girls both clammed up. They all sipped their coffee and chewed on their biscuits. Then suddenly Bradley stood up and winked in Jillian's direction. "Well, I'm off," he announced. "Early meeting in the morning. Do you want to come up and get that book I was telling you about?"

'What book' was on the tip of her tongue before she twigged. But she found herself wondering whether he wanted to spend time alone with her or was just providing the opportunity for Imogen and Grant to have some quality time together. Hopefully both. Feeling suddenly quite randy, Jillian said goodnight to Grant and went upstairs with her boyfriend.

As the door closed behind them, the room went very quiet. Imogen shifted nervously in her seat and then gathered up the coffee mugs and took them to the kitchen. Grant followed her in. "I heard the two of you talking when you were making the coffee," he now revealed. Imogen looked at him questioningly, trying to remember what they had said. "Jillian called me a mummy's boy."

"I'm sure she didn't mean any harm by it."

"She told you to be careful."

"I can look after myself."

Grant smiled at her nervously. "I don't actually blame her," he said, "but I'd like to explain. I gave something to my mum tonight and she got a bit emotional, Robyn too. We wouldn't normally behave like that in public, or even in private for that matter."

"Gave her something?"

Grant just held out his left hand and wiggled his fingers in her direction.

Imogen gasped. "You're not wearing your ring!"

He took her in his arms and kissed her. "Time to move on," he declared. "I hope that a new chapter in my life has started tonight."

"I hope so too."

"You don't already have a boyfriend or anything?"

"No."

"Have you ever been in a serious relationship? I can't believe you haven't been snapped up."

"I've been clinging on to a memory," Imogen admitted. "I was with someone for over a year. I thought I was happy with him but he let me down badly and I realise now that it would never have worked. His name was Sam. But he's history now; I don't miss him one bit."

As Grant kissed her again she felt her heart burst with joy because she knew that those words she had just spoken were true. She really had got over her failed relationship with Sam. Tania was welcome to him. She even felt magnanimous enough to hope that they would gel properly as a couple and find happiness with the child they were expecting. No hard feelings.

Imogen heard a buzz from her phone as a text message came through. She ignored it and returned the kiss, her head dizzy with happiness.

"You'd better check that," Grant said when they finally came out of their embrace. He hoped it was not something that would spoil the mood. He needn't have worried. The text was from Jillian.

See you in the morning xx

"Now why should she have all the fun?" Imogen asked seductively as she showed the message to Grant.

"I couldn't agree more," he replied. And they kissed again.

Chapter 12

A week flew by with unbelievable speed. Imogen had never been so happy in her life and it was obvious that things were also going to plan for Jillian. What good fortune they had both encountered since moving into this flat. Now the preparations for Christmas were in full swing and they had given their joint living space a festive feel with a small decorated tree and some scented candles. Imogen had added a fluffy reindeer and two penguins in her own room. It was Saturday morning.

"You sleeping upstairs again tonight?" Imogen mused, making it sound more like a fait accompli than a question.

"Well, I suppose I might get some sleep," Jillian answered with a cheeky grin. "Grant staying over?"

"Mmm." Imogen licked her lips in anticipation.

"How's your blog going? You haven't mentioned it much recently."

"It's just like you said," she now admitted to her friend. "I can't really be bothered with it at the moment. I'm too busy living a real life with real people."

"And what about your mum's diary?"

Imogen let out a big sigh. "You know what?" she pronounced. "I don't care about that any more either. It's none of my business. Everyone has secrets from the past and that's what they should remain. Secrets. If it was anything of any importance my mum would have told me about it. What about you? How are you getting on with Maggie?"

"Great," Jillian answered. "I think this is going to be one of my best issues to date. I watched her teach one of her sessions yesterday. She was doing the **er** sound."

"That's 'er' as in 'super' or 'worker', right?"

"Yes, but think again. There are other possibilities."

Imogen scratched her head. "Peter, sister, longer, shorter. It's always 'er'."

"What about 'girl' or 'bird'?" suggested Jillian.

"Oh yes, that does make the same sound but it's 'ir'. Still, that's only two."

"So how do you spell 'sailor' or 'doctor'?"

Imogen thought about it and then agreed that the 'or' in those words sounds exactly the same as the 'er' or the 'ir' in the others. "I see what you mean," she concurred. "It *is* quite fascinating. But what ever happened to long and short vowels and silent letters? I can't remember how I learnt to spell but this method seems quite new to me. Mind you, lots of people do have great difficulty with spelling so maybe this would make them think about it."

"That's the whole idea, to make people more aware of how words are made up of sounds. But there's no easy way of deciding why one representation of the sound works in any particular instance. For example why not 'sistor' or 'docter'?"

"It just wouldn't look right but only because we are used to seeing the correct spelling."

"Exactly. So that's three ways to spell **er**. Can you think of any others?"

"There are more?"

"Spell 'pillar'."

Imogen nodded. "Right, that's 'ar'."

"Curly."

"So 'ur' works as well. That's actually all the vowels."

"Lyrics."

"OK, you're going to give me a headache now. You can make the same sound with 'yr' and not use a vowel at all. So we're up to six possibilities. There can't be more than that."

Jillian laughed. "Your face is a picture," she said. "There are a few more like 'our' as in 'colour', 'ear' as in 'early', 'orr' as in 'worry' and so on."

"Maggie must be very proud of you picking it all up so quickly."

"She did say that I was a good pupil. 'Urr' is another one; think of 'curry' or 'hurry'."

"Well, good luck with writing the article. I hope your readers will be suitably impressed."

"Me too. It could go pear-shaped and bore people to tears but Maggie is a fully qualified teacher and knows what she's talking about. She's actually looking for a full-time teaching job but they seem to be hard to come by at the moment so she's taking these part-time classes in the interim and also doing some substitute work. So fingers crossed for her that she'll find a job and fingers crossed for me that the article goes down well. The architecture issue seems to be selling quite well."

Their conversation was ended by the sound of the doorbell and there was Grant in his winter woollies ready for the planned visit to the Christmas Continental Market in the grounds of the City Hall. Imogen grabbed her own coat and accompanied him out to the car.

"I've got two hours," he told her. "I'm working the late shift from four-thirty until nine."

"No mulled wine for you then," she quipped, clicking her seat-belt into place.

"No, but *you* can still have some."

Imogen smiled. She loved the atmosphere of the market. The sights and sounds and especially the smells of the olives, cheeses and salamis always reminded her of the happy holidays she had spent in France when she was younger. She was intending to visit some of those stalls today and choose something special for a tasty supper. Grant had promised to come straight round after work and she could hardly wait for a repeat performance of their night of passion. Last week had been wonderful. They parked the car and walked round to the City Hall to join the throngs of people already there, many of them munching hot dogs and burgers. Imogen headed for the Italian breads first and bought some of those. They smelt delicious. She was just deciding which type of olives looked the most appetising when she heard her name called out from a few stalls away.

"It's that couple over there," advised Grant. "They're both waving at you."

Imogen looked in the direction he was pointing and spotted her own parents. She ran over, pulling Grant with her by the arm. Joanna gave her a hug and Keith grinned at her.

"Grant," she said a bit nervously, "this is my mum, Joanna and my dad, Keith." And then addressing her parents she added, "This is Grant, Grant Cartwright."

There was a lot of hand shaking and pleasantries were exchanged, followed by a bit of small talk about the weather and the surrounding market produce. Then her parents looked as though they were ready to move on. But suddenly Joanna asked Imogen about Christmas Day. "You're still coming to us for dinner, aren't you," she quizzed.

"Yes, of course," Imogen replied. She could sense her mother relaxing.

"Oh, good. It's just that, well, you are of course welcome to bring a guest. If you want. I mean, if you and…"

"OK, thanks Mum."

"You'd be very welcome, Grant."

"We'll let you know." Imogen was at once grateful for the invitation and embarrassed for Grant. They'd only known each other for two weeks. But her mother had obviously realised at a glance that he was no casual acquaintance.

"I'd love to come, Mrs Tomlinson," Grant then replied, squeezing Imogen's hand. "Thank you very much for asking me. I'm sure my own mother won't mind as she'll have my two sisters for company. We can have a special meal with her some other day that week."

"Oh, that's brilliant," Imogen's mum beamed at them both. "But it's Joanna and Keith. No need for any formality."

They parted and went their separate ways. Imogen went back to the olive stall with a spring in her step. She made her purchase and then turned round to find Grant now chatting to someone else, a very pretty girl with long, blonde hair. But he didn't introduce her. As soon as he saw Imogen coming he gave the other girl a hug and waved her good-bye. She took a curious glance at Imogen and moved away.

"Don't tell me. An old flame," Imogen said, dispirited. She wished that one of her own former boyfriends would suddenly appear just so that they could be even. She had to admit to a slight feeling of envy.

"Actually, she's Zoe's sister, Erica," Grant announced without further ado. He just stated it as a matter of fact, didn't look the least bit upset.

"Oh, she had a sister! God, I'm sorry. Talk about putting my foot in it."

Grant just smiled and took her hand again. They strolled over to the drinks tent to get her a glass of mulled wine. It would soon be time to go back to the car.

★★★

The evening panned out exactly as Imogen had dared to anticipate. Bradley called in for a drink and engaged in some small talk before escorting Jillian upstairs for dinner. Not only did she take her handbag this time but also her toothbrush and one or two other essentials. Imogen knew that she wouldn't see her friend until the morning or maybe even the afternoon. It was patently obvious that they couldn't wait to get their hands on one another. And that left the path clear for her own lovemaking. As the door closed behind them, Imogen set to work. She laid the table with candles and flowers, stocked the fridge with white wine and Champagne, and began to prepare a meal using the fresh market produce she had purchased. Grant was working late so she understood that he wouldn't want anything too heavy. She opted for a tapas type menu with little bowls of marinated olives, sundried tomatoes and pickled beetroot along with several cheeses, all served with a selection of potato crisps and Italian breads. She dimmed the lights so that the Christmas tree was the main focus of illumination and then went to the bathroom for a shower. Checking the time, she changed into her sexiest dress and sprayed herself with her favourite Chanel perfume. Her timing was perfect; the doorbell rang just as she emerged from her bedroom.

Grant took one look at the romantic surroundings and melted into her arms.

"You smell delicious," he cooed, kissing her on the lips.

Imogen breathed in his manly scent and guided him to the sofa. She handed him a glass of wine and sat down beside him. Grant took one big sip and then set the glass down on the nearby table. He looked her straight in the eye. "You don't know what this means to me," he told her, "to come home to such a lovely warm welcome."

"Are you hungry?" she asked him in response.

He grinned at her. "I'm hungry for you," he decreed. "What are you trying to do to me, wearing that provocative dress and no stockings? You look gorgeous."

"I just wanted to look nice for you," she answered demurely. But even as she said it she was inching closer to him. He reached out and touched her lightly, just above the knee. Imogen savoured the sensation and felt her whole body tingle with excitement. Her head was swimming with happiness and desire but somehow she managed to control her impulses, telling herself it would be even better later on as their yearning for each other intensifies. "Let's eat first," she proposed, leading him to the table.

The tapas meal was a huge success and nicely washed down with a bottle of Chardonnay followed by a glass of sparkling Prosecco. Once again they relaxed on the sofa, allowing the food to settle while they listened to the new Coldplay CD playing in the background. A buzz from her phone alerted Imogen to a message coming through.

Imogen, it's Holly. Thought you would want to know. Tania has had her baby. It's a boy.

Imogen handed the phone to Grant so that he could read it too; she had filled him in on her romantic history during the week. Then she replied to the girl who used to be her friend.

Thanks for letting me know.

An answer came back right away.

No problem. Do you still love him? I never did say sorry.

Imogen felt angry for just a moment. Then she glanced at Grant and her heart melted. She sent another reply.

No, you didn't. But it doesn't matter anymore.

The phone buzzed again.

Sorry.

"She's reaching out to you," Grant said. "Why don't you make your peace with her? Life is too short for grudges and recriminations."

Imogen smiled at him and thought about his words. He knew all about life being too short. She sent Holly a longer message.

I really appreciate you keeping me informed, Holly. But I meant what I said. I was just having a bad day that time I phoned you up. I am well over Sam and hope he is happy with Tania.

I hope that you have managed to move on as well. He treated both of us badly. It would be nice if we could be friends again.

She didn't have to wait long for a response.

I'd like that. As long as you don't talk about Sam.

"Poor Holly. She's obviously upset." Imogen keyed in a short reply.

Sam who?

She imagined the smile on Holly's face as the answer came through.

Lol I've missed you, Imogen xx

Grant put his arm round her as she ended the line of communication.

Me too. But I have to go now before my boyfriend gets bored. See you soon xx

The music had ended. They both enjoyed the quiet stillness and shared a kiss.

"I liked your parents," Grant remarked after a while. "It was nice of them to ask me to Christmas dinner."

"Are you sure your mum won't mind?"

"She'll understand. I want to spend the day with you.

And she won't be on her own so there isn't a problem."

Imogen sighed with contentment. She loved her parents and she knew she was falling in love with Grant. She wanted them to like each other. But niggling somewhere at the back of her mind was a slight worry about that diary entry. She was no closer to solving the mystery of what had taken place that November day back in 1990 when she was just three years old, but she was closer to realising that she could not just pass it off as something that was none of her business. She had to know. Instinctively she sensed that whatever it was would eventually have an important bearing on her own life and on her relationship with her mother.

"Let's go to bed," Grant whispered in her ear. She put the diary from her mind and held her breath as he slowly unzipped her dress and eased it from her shoulders and down over her slim well-toned legs. As she stepped out of it exposing her pretty pink bra and knickers she began to unbutton his pink and grey striped shirt. And suddenly his hands were everywhere and she was loving it. They went to bed leaving their clothes strewn across the floor. And the sex was wonderful. Imogen didn't want that feeling of ecstasy to ever come to an end.

Chapter 13

She knew that she hadn't got the job when she didn't receive a phone call that Tuesday morning two weeks ago but now the official letter arrived. Maggie opened it despondently and read those familiar words. 'The governors are sorry to inform you …', 'Thanks for your interest' and other well-worn platitudes. As she read it more thoroughly, however, she learnt that on this occasion she had impressed the interview panel and had actually been placed as first reserve in the event of the successful candidate not taking up the position. That wasn't likely to happen but it was at least an accolade of sorts and gave her a good feeling. The letter went on to say that the standard of interview had been extremely high and that she should be proud of her performance. It ended by wishing her well in future applications.

Maggie phoned Uncle Bill to give him the news. He had been so supportive of her through the years and particularly in recent times with her studies and job applications that she felt he deserved to have the feedback.

"Well done," he told her in a cheery voice. "There must be one with your name on it coming up soon."

Maggie smiled. Thank goodness for his positive attitudes. If only her dad could have been more like her mum's brother. Uncle Bill had been a tower of strength since her dad had upped and left when she was just a little girl. It still pained her to think about that event and she couldn't help holding herself responsible. Married at twenty-two with a baby already on the way was always going to be an inauspicious start to family life. He was obviously too young for fatherhood and simply couldn't cope. But he could have tried harder. He could have been a better dad.

Lawrence arrived while she was still thinking about her parents. He read the letter and handed it back to her with a smile. "You obviously did yourself proud in that interview," he told her. "Why the long face? You already knew you didn't get the job."

"I was just ruminating on my dad's attitudes, as usual," Maggie answered with a sigh.

"Why? What has he said? I'm really fed up with that man upsetting you."

Maggie quickly explained that he hadn't said anything; he didn't even know about this particular application. She had just been making comparisons in her mind between her dad and her uncle. Lawrence gave her a hug. "Don't let him get you down, Mags," he said wisely. "He isn't worth it."

"That's easier said than done," she retorted.

"Well, let's see about that," he replied with a twinkle

in his eye. And he kissed her. It was like magic, instantly dispelling the gloom. "I love you, Mags. That's all that matters."

"I love you too," Maggie whispered in his ear and she kissed him back.

Chapter 14

Bradley decided to surprise Jillian with a pre-Christmas shopping and sight-seeing trip to London. She was over the moon. Leaving young Ben in charge of the magazine for a few days, she flew out from the George Best Belfast City Airport with Bradley early on Thursday morning. They were in the centre of London in time for lunch.

"Stop worrying and just enjoy yourself," Bradley laughed as she checked whether there were any messages from Ben.

"I'm not worried," she defended herself. "It's just that I've never left Ben in the office on his own before for two whole days. But he'll be fine. He'll probably relish the freedom to go mad with his graphics. The new edition is almost ready for printing."

"No more interviews or lesson observations with Maggie then?" He too had been on the receiving end of a lot of spelling advice, just like Imogen.

"I'm going to miss that," she confessed. "It has definitely made me think more about how words are constructed. I mean, did you ever really think about it before, how 'sion' and 'tion' both make the same sound, just like 'shun'."

"Here we go again," Bradley replied, pretending to yawn with boredom.

She nudged him playfully with her elbow and laughed. "I can't help it. It fascinates me."

She put her phone away and asked whether Bradley was quite confident that his business would cope without him for the unexpected days off.

"Nobody is indispensable," he pronounced wisely with a smirk. "Nigel will be glad that I owe him one."

They both relaxed and perused the menu, agreeing to have something light and a proper dinner later on. Bradley chose a burger and Jillian a pappardelle dish with roasted red peppers and pine nuts. They shared a bottle of wine. And then they were off for a whirlwind tour of the city, enjoying a ride on the London Eye. Luckily the sky was fairly clear with just a few clouds dotted here and there so they got a good view and were able to pick out several well-known landmarks. After a stroll through Covent Garden and some shopping in Oxford Street they returned to their hotel, laden with several bags and parcels. Jillian slumped down into the chair by the window and kicked her shoes off, sighing with relief. Bradley stretched out on the bed and yawned.

"I can hardly believe that I didn't even know you a few weeks ago," he then said with a smile. "This just feels so right and so good, spending time together like this."

Jillian moved over to join him on the bed and they lay

in each other's arms, savouring the moment. "I know," she said. "I love it too."

Bradley leaned across and lifted an envelope he had placed on the bedside table. "Look what I've got," he announced, producing tickets for the musical, *Beautiful*. "I thought we should go to a show and figured you'd enjoy this one. We need to get ready now if we're going to have time to eat first."

And so their fairy-tale trip continued with a superb meal, a romantic show and a passionate night together in the hotel. Jillian loved every minute of it and she loved Bradley more and more with every second that they spent together. Life couldn't get much better.

★★★

Back home in Belfast and still on an emotional high, Jillian went to Bradley's flat and helped him to wrap the presents he had bought for his own family and for Alastair, Gertrude and Thomasina. They had decided to split their time on Christmas Day between their own two families so the presents for Alastair and his mother and grandmother would have to be delivered before that. With only a week to go, it made sense to do that right away so they got everything into the car and off they went to Gertrude's house.

"Do you never visit Alastair in his own home?" Jillian enquired as they headed down the dual carriageway.

"I have been there a couple of times," Bradley answered, "but Gertrude is definitely the focal point of their family and events are always held at her place. I know they'll all be going there for Christmas."

"They seem to be a very close family, very supportive of each other."

"There's no doubt about that," agreed Bradley.

There were several cars already parked in the driveway and Jillian was a bit reluctant to go in. She was afraid of interrupting something or being met by a sea of unfamiliar faces but Bradley was adamant that they had made the journey now and might as well complete their mission; they didn't need to stay long. He rang the doorbell.

"Hi Bradley, come on in." It was Alastair's cousin, Robyn. She smiled at Jillian, remembering her from the party three weeks ago.

"We're not disturbing you, are we?" Bradley asked her. "You seem to have quite a few visitors already."

"All here to talk about me!" she exclaimed with a grunt. "As if I'm not old enough to make my own decisions."

"Why, what have you done?" laughed Bradley, catching sight of a couple of men in the house for a change.

They followed Robyn into the kitchen where she introduced them to her boyfriend, Jack and Jack's older brother, Luke, who had apparently given him a lift over and hadn't yet managed to 'make his escape' due to the 'interrogation' he was receiving from her mother, her aunt, her granny and even her dad.

"Your dad?" quizzed Bradley in surprise.

"Yes," she quipped in an exasperated tone. "He just happened to be here when Jack arrived so he had to put in his two pennyworth. It's so embarrassing. I didn't even expect Mum to be here let alone Dad. That's why I arranged to meet Jack here in the first place and not at home."

Jillian laughed, recognising the tactics as something she might have done herself in the past.

"Why is he here?" Bradley asked, confused. "I didn't think your parents were in touch with one another. Or not much anyway."

"Dropping off Christmas presents," Robyn explained.

"Same as us then," Bradley rejoined. "I'll just leave these things under your gran's tree if that's all right. Is Alastair here too?"

"No, he's at work," she answered. "Garden centres with gift shops are very busy at this time of the year, even on Saturdays."

"Of course," Jillian agreed, nodding.

Suddenly there was a flurry of activity as Gertrude and Thomasina realised who the newcomers were. As usual they made a big fuss of welcoming Bradley which gave Luke the opportunity to slip out the back and drive off. Bradley handed over the presents. Thomasina gave Jillian a hug.

"It's lovely to see you again," she told her. "You and Bradley make a fine pair." Then she turned to Bradley. "Thanks for these. There are also some gifts for you under the tree. Make sure you don't go without them."

"So what's going on with Robyn?" Bradley asked her.

Thomasina sighed, then smiled as she led them into the sitting room. "It's quite funny really," she proclaimed.

"Catherine has been seeing quite a lot of Robyn's dad lately but she isn't sure whether it's leading anywhere or not and didn't want to get Robyn's hopes up so she arranged to meet him here instead of at their own house. But no sooner had she arrived than Robyn turned up herself, having arranged to meet her new boyfriend here! Neither Catherine nor Mark knew anything about Robyn having a boyfriend and are obviously a bit concerned about the furtive way she was going about things so they have both been giving the poor boy the third degree. He actually appears to be perfectly respectable."

Bradley laughed. "I don't think she has realised that her parents were deliberately arranging a meeting," he assured her. "She told us that her dad had just turned up with Christmas presents."

"Good," Thomasina said, pleased that the ruse had been accepted by her niece. "She has been dreaming of her parents getting back together for years."

"Do you think it might happen?" Jillian asked.

"It's starting to look that way."

"Wow! That would be so romantic. Don't worry, we won't say a word."

As the barrage of questions continued in the next room, they all began to feel a bit sorry for young Jack. Then suddenly Thomasina was speaking again.

"This will be my twenty-sixth Christmas without Raymond. I still miss him every day."

"Christmas must be particularly difficult," Jillian sympathised, realising that Raymond must have been Alastair's father.

"It is," Thomasina agreed, "especially when the accident happened at this time of year." She paused before continuing. "But I think I have cocooned myself from reality for far too long. Grant has made me sit up and take stock. The way he has bounced back after Zoe is wonderful. None of us would have wanted him to be miserable all of his life. And now Catherine is considering taking a risk with Mark. I hope she does. Maybe it's not too late for me, after all."

"You've had your hands full with Alastair," Bradley reminded her.

"It's not just that," Thomasina declared. "The most difficult part has always been the lack of closure; the anger and bitterness that just won't go away."

"Because there was no-one to blame?" Bradley had always understood that this aspect of the incident had troubled the family the most.

Jillian looked confused. "I've never heard what actually happened," she said. "Was the other driver killed too?"

Bradley took her hand and squeezed it in support as he explained. "Alastair and his father weren't in a car. They were walking along a country lane and a car hit them. It just drove off, never to be seen again."

Jillian felt a cold shiver run through her body. "Oh no," she exclaimed. "I hadn't realised. It was a hit and run! I had always assumed that two cars had collided or something. Gosh, that's dreadful. Were there no witnesses?"

Thomasina shook her head. "There was another

family who saw the car speeding away but they were so shocked that they didn't manage to recall any details."

Just then Gertrude arrived with coffee and a tray containing mince pies and other seasonal treats and Robyn came running in to say good-bye. Her parents had finally agreed that they had no problem with her going out with Jack. Immediately the conversation took on a lighter tone and even Thomasina seemed to relax and enjoy herself as they all sipped their coffees and sampled the nibbles. Jillian was more proud of Bradley than ever; all those years ago he had befriended a family in crisis and it was so obvious to her that, right up to the present day, they really appreciated his support. What a hideous thing to have happened.

Chapter 15

Imogen loved her independent life since moving to her own apartment in October but it felt right being back home with her mum and dad for Christmas. She had really enjoyed the day especially having Grant with her; he had given her the most beautiful silver and amethyst bracelet along with a gorgeous silk scarf and some of her favourite shower gel. He had also brought chocolates and flowers for her mum and a bottle of port for her dad and they had both agreed that he was charming. Joanna's parents had also had lunch with them, bringing back memories of Christmases past when they would also have been joined by Annie and Don. But they were happy memories and they didn't dwell on the fact that they were no longer around. Imogen promised to have her grandparents round soon to visit her flat and they had both indicated that they would be delighted to come and that they very much approved of Grant, declaring him to be a real gentleman. They had left a couple of hours ago to spend the evening with friends.

It was now Imogen's favourite time of day. Dinner

was over, the table was cleared, the presents had been opened and the debris had been tidied away; wrapping paper, empty boxes, pulled crackers and so on. The red cinnamon and juniper candles still burned on the table, their flickering light casting moving shadows around the room whilst the yule logs burned brightly in the fireplace creating a warm, cosy atmosphere. The television was on in the corner but no-one was watching it any longer. Plates had been piled high with roast turkey, ham, sausages wrapped in bacon, stuffing, vegetables, roast potatoes and gravy, not to mention the soup to start with and the plum pudding with brandy sauce for dessert. Large quantities of red wine had been consumed. Now they were all feeling very snoozy and eyelids were beginning to droop. Imogen had twice jerked herself awake as she felt herself dropping off but this third time she glanced around the room and realised that everyone else had given up fighting against it; they were all fast asleep and gently snoring. She lifted a sweet from the bowl of Quality Street and unwrapped it. It was her favourite, a strawberry cream. Popping it in her mouth, she observed yet again the tastefully decorated tree and the artistic way her mother had arranged all the cards she had received from friends and relatives.

Imogen believed it was a shame that some people were moving away from the tradition of sending Christmas cards. Even she, who used social media as much as most, loved to see the postman arriving in the run-up to the big day and the bigger the pile of envelopes he delivered the better. It was a chance to catch up with people from the past, people you don't see from one year's end to the next and yet you don't want them to disappear from your life. They evoke memories. And there is often a note included or even a full letter or a photograph or two. Imogen's childhood friend, Jimmy, was a case in point. Having searched him out for old times' sake she had discovered that he was now in America and they had exchanged cards. Even though he had already posted pictures of himself and his family on Facebook, she had been quite excited to receive his Christmas card; it was so much more personal. Even the cards from people you do see regularly bring a smile to your face, she now surmised, and they help to make the house look festive with all the cheery robins, snowmen and glittery Victorian scenes. Imogen sighed. The growing trend to give a donation to charity instead was all very well in itself but she couldn't see any reason why people couldn't do both. For the majority of the population who had gone down this route it had nothing to do with saving the planet or with money; it wasn't as if they could only afford one of the options and the paper used could always be recycled. But she had to accept that old traditions eventually die out and new ones are born and that some folk just can't be bothered any more. She took a deep breath. There was a lovely spicy aroma in the air, partly from the scented candles and partly from the lovely meal they had eaten. Before she would once again succumb to sleep, Imogen rose out of her seat to stretch her legs. And suddenly she had an idea.

The staircase creaked, the sound of every step magnified in Imogen's mind, as she guiltily made her way to the wardrobe in her parents' bedroom. She knew that she shouldn't be doing this. It was dishonest and sneaky. But she couldn't let this opportunity slip by. They were all asleep. No-one would know. She tiptoed into the room and opened the wardrobe. She removed all the jumpers from the front of the bottom shelf. And there they were, her mother's diaries. She went back out onto the landing and leaned over the banister, listening for any movement. Nothing.

Back in the bedroom Imogen got down on her knees and reached in to pull out a pile of books. There were two in front of all the others, 1987 and 1991. Those were the ones she had already borrowed and returned. She still had the 1989 and 1993 diaries at the flat. There was one with a little padlock covering the years from 1971 to 1975; Joanna would only have been ten when she started that one. She checked the other dates; 1978, 1979, 1976, 1983, 1984, 1990. 1990! She had the book she was looking for in her hands! Carefully she replaced all the others and shoved the jumpers back in front just as she heard a door opening downstairs. A sense of panic gripped her. She mustn't be caught. Today of all days, after the lovely time they had all spent in each other's company. As quietly as she could, Imogen closed the wardrobe door and tiptoed out of the room, stuffing the book under her sweater. She knew she was going to be seen so she went straight to the bathroom and made a fuss of flushing the toilet as loudly as possible before running down the stairs with heavy footsteps.

"What are you doing up there?" Joanna asked in

surprise, still looking only half awake. There was a perfectly good toilet on the ground floor.

"You were all asleep," Imogen replied, "so I used the upstairs loo in case I would waken anyone."

She hated lying to her mother but her excuse was instantly accepted.

"That was very considerate," the older woman remarked. "Would you like another cup of tea?"

"Coffee would be great," Imogen answered her, leaving Joanna to go into the kitchen whilst she returned to the lounge and slipped the diary into her handbag. Luckily she had chosen to carry quite a large bag for a change; she often used a fairly small one. It crossed her mind that maybe, in her subconscious, she had intended to do that all along, catch the others asleep and rummage through the wardrobe. She glanced across at Grant. He was just opening his eyes. Hopefully he had not seen her secrete the book in her bag because she didn't want him to draw the others' attention to it, nor did she even want to explain her actions to him. Much as she would love to have been able to confide in Grant and would have done about anything else, something had stopped her in this instance. These were her own parents she was investigating and it was surely bad enough that she had blurted out things to Jillian. She already felt disloyal enough without involving Grant as well. Thankfully he didn't seem to have noticed anything. He just smiled at her sleepily and blew her a kiss. Then, with a yawn, he stretched his arms and checked his watch.

"Gosh, is that the time?" he said. "Thomasina will be

here for me soon." Grant's aunt had drawn the short straw and agreed to do driver for the day. Imogen had three choices. She could stay with her parents, she could go to Granny Gertrude's for an hour or two with Grant or she could go home; Thomasina would drop her off. Now that the elusive diary was in her grip, she would really have preferred to go for the last option; she could hardly wait to read the solution to the mystery. But spending some more time in Grant's company was too compelling. And she thought it was only fair to accompany him to his family gathering when he had spent the bulk of the day with hers. So she drank her coffee and prepared to go with him.

"Don't be a stranger," Keith said to Grant as they put their coats on ready for the icy blast outside. "It's been good having another man in the house today."

"I'll definitely be back," Grant replied. "It's been a great day. Thank you for inviting me."

There were smiles and hugs and handshakes all around and then they were off, chatting to Thomasina in the car, their gifts neatly stored in the boot. She was playing a CD of festive tunes and wearing a paper hat that she had obviously got in a cracker earlier in the day. A light flurry of snow was adding to the Christmassy atmosphere. Imogen and Grant sat together in the back seat, arms round each other for warmth. Imogen instantly forgot about her mission to solve a mystery from the past. This was fun. She was with the man she loves. Loves? She realised with a start that yes, it was definitely love she felt for Grant and she knew it was reciprocated.

She sincerely hoped it would last a lifetime. As though reading her mind, Grant held her closer and kissed her full on the lips.

"Hey, behave yourselves in the back there," Thomasina called out. "I have a mirror you know."

And all three of them burst out laughing.

★★★

In bed that night, back in her own apartment, Imogen reflected on the happiest Christmas she had spent for a long time. Grant had come home with her after a couple of hours of fun and games in his grandmother's cottage with Rebecca, Robyn and Alastair. There had been more eating and drinking. In fact they were both feeling quite tipsy when they got home. Which made Grant even more amorous and more adventurous in the bedroom. Imogen lapped it up with relish. And then he said those magic words. "I love you, Imogen. I absolutely love and adore you. You are the best thing that has ever happened to me." She waited. He was sure to mention Zoe and the moment would be spoilt. But he didn't. And then she felt a pang of guilt and imagined herself in Zoe's position. Life goes on.

"I love you too," she gushed, unable now to control herself. "I love you so much, Grant." She closed her eyes and groaned, revelling in the sensation of his touch, at once utterly divine yet almost unbearable. "Again," she mouthed, breathing rapidly and wanting more. And he didn't disappoint. Pure bliss. What a perfect end to a wonderful day.

Chapter 16

Jillian was spending the day with Bradley. Grant had to go to work. He had left early to get freshened up at home and to change into his work clothes. Imogen had the place to herself. Perfect. Her mum's diary was still in her handbag and the mounting anticipation was palpable as she contemplated reading it. Should she go straight to that page or should she try to get a flavour of the year first, see if there was anything leading up to the big revelation? She decided to savour the moment. She had all day. Why rush to the finale?

She got up and made breakfast, toasted pancakes and coffee. After the amount of food and drink she had consumed the previous day that would be more than enough. She had really enjoyed herself. Her parents had liked Grant, his family had been friendly towards her and the quality time spent together to round off the day had been sensational. Now, at last, she was going to find out what had happened to make her mother write those curious entries in her diary. She took the book from her bag and went back to bed.

It was very tempting to turn straightaway to November but she controlled that urge. She opened it at the first page.

The beginning of a new year. I wonder what it has in store. Keith has hinted that he'd like us to have another baby. I would love that. After all Imogen will be three in October. Maybe start trying soon!

Wow! Imogen wondered what had gone wrong there. They never did produce a sibling for her. She moved on a few pages.

Mum and Dad came round to look after Imogen so Keith and I could get away for the weekend. What a luxury!! Though I am really going to miss her. But it's only for two nights. She'll be fine.

And on the next page:

My husband is the most romantic hunk imaginable!!! I am having the time of my life. This hotel is the height of indulgence and we are making the most of it. We had such fun last night in the king-size bed – nudge, nudge, wink, wink.

"Oops!" Imogen said aloud. This was a bit embarrassing and she felt her face going red. But it was also very heart-warming. She could resist it no longer. It was time to read what Joanna had written on 10th November. Tentatively she turned the pages with her heart in her mouth. She glanced at the entries for the 7th, 8th, 9th – nothing unusual there. But where was 10th? Or the 11th, 12th and 13th for that matter. The pages were missing!

That was the last thing on earth that Imogen had expected to find. She began to sweat profusely and breathe very heavily. It must be something bad, something really bad for her mother to have torn it out. She felt sick. Why could she not have stuck to her resolve to let well alone? What was she to do now? Glancing across at the right hand side of the diary, she read what Joanna had written for the 14th.

Will my life ever be the same again? We can hardly look at each other.

The tone of the diary changed dramatically from that day onwards. The happy carefree comments had vanished to be replaced by a terse record of routine events. Imogen flicked from page to page, bewildered and frustrated. What a disappointment! She set the book down and closed her eyes, hoping for inspiration. She had accumulated quite a comprehensive account of the year. Two of her favourite films had been released, *Ghost* and *Pretty Woman*. Ayrton Senna had won the Grand Prix. West Germany had won the FIFA World Cup, beating Argentina in the final. Stefan Edberg had beaten Boris Becker in the Wimbledon final with the women's title going to Martina Navratilova. But nothing to explain why Joanna appeared to be depressed in the latter part of the year. Imogen could have cried as she read the last entry in the book:

Keith is still sleeping in the spare room. I love him so much and I know he loves me but we can't get past the guilt. We are both accountable for what happened that night but keeping that hideous secret is slowly killing me.

So they were both at fault. But what did they do? Imogen would never be able to look at her parents again without scrutinising their behaviour for clues. She recalled what she had read before; it had something to do with a little boy. That gave her a very uncomfortable feeling. One way or another, her duvet day was ruined; she got up and got dressed.

No longer at ease with her own company, Imogen turned on the TV and tried to relax. But the news from across the water was so depressing. Hundreds of people flooded out of their homes. Rescue boats being paddled along what should have been major roads, now turned into muddy rivers. Bridges swept away like matchsticks. A feeling of selfishness gnawed at her conscience as she recalled the comfortable day she had spent in the lap of luxury whilst these poor people were struggling to salvage the bare necessities of life. She turned it off. But it had made her think. Why was she worrying about a stupid diary? In the greater scheme of things there were more important issues in life and she should be grateful for the good fortune that had given her pretty well everything she needed. She started to do a Sudoku puzzle, deliberately choosing a 'super fiendish' one so that she would have to give it her full concentration. It took her over an hour but she managed to complete it and the mental activity did take her mind off other things. She was just enjoying the well-earned sense of achievement when she heard a car door slam outside and excited voices rang out in the foyer.

The door flew open and Jillian burst in like a breath of fresh air, closely followed by Bradley. They had been to the sales and were each carrying two large carrier bags.

"You won't believe the bargains we've found!" Jillian exclaimed, pulling a lovely quilted gilet from the first bag and holding it up for her friend to admire.

"That's gorgeous," Imogen agreed. "What's in the other bag?"

"Two pairs of shoes."

Bradley slumped down onto the sofa, keeping his own purchases to himself. "We've come back to see if you'd like to join us for lunch," he announced. "With Grant working all day we figured you might be at a loose end."

Imogen perked up immediately. What lovely considerate friends she had. And what better way was there to cast those niggling worries from her mind. She was ready in a flash and they all made their way back into town. They found a free table in their favourite wine bar and ordered a sharing platter of mixed tapas. It came with the usual salamis and cheeses but also had little strips of turkey and small sausages and an extra cranberry dip in honour of the season. They also shared a bottle of refreshing white wine.

It was Jillian who first noticed the couple sitting a few tables away. She nudged Imogen and nodded in their direction. "Isn't that Grant's mother over there?" Imogen glanced across and she too recognised Catherine looking very cosy and intimate with a smart yet casually dressed gentleman in a blue sweater with a snowman motif. They were staring into each other's eyes like young lovers, oblivious to the other diners in the room.

"I think that's Robyn's dad she's with," Jillian added. "We saw him at the house one day although we weren't actually introduced."

"That's right," put in Bradley, also recognising the pair. "I think he's called Mark."

Imogen continued to observe her boyfriend's mother and her partner for a few moments until Catherine suddenly glanced in her direction and spotted her. Waving a hand in recognition, the older woman turned to her gentleman friend and whispered something in his ear. He then gave Imogen a warm smile. Embarrassed at being caught out watching them, Imogen turned away and took a sip of her wine. But suddenly Catherine was at her shoulder, a happy glint in her eye.

"Would you do me a big favour," she requested, addressing all three of them, "and not tell Grant that you saw us together."

Imogen wasn't sure that she wanted to make that promise. If she was going to make a life with Grant she wanted him to be able to wholly trust her just as she wanted to know that she could trust him. They shouldn't be keeping secrets from each other. Even though she was still keeping a big one. But then, accurately reading her mind, Catherine qualified her remark:

"You see, Mark and I have some big news and we would rather tell him ourselves. We're getting married."

Well that certainly put a different slant on it. Of course an announcement of that magnitude should come straight from his mother.

"I won't say a word," Imogen avowed, smiling, "and neither will my friends."

"Of course not," chorused Jillian and Bradley. "And congratulations."

"Thank you."

"Does Robyn know yet?" asked Imogen.

"Nobody does. Only you."

All three jumped out of their seats at this news to give Catherine a hug, then moved across to shake Mark by the hand. Imogen felt proud that Catherine had confided in her.

It shows that she likes me and accepts me as part of the family. Or maybe she was just scared that I'd put two and two together and work it out for myself so she had to tell me so that I wouldn't steal her thunder. But whatever the reason, I hope she tells Grant soon because it'll be hard to keep this from him for any length of time. And I hope that Grant will be happy for her because Mark may be Robyn's dad but he's not his. I'm not sure how he'll feel about it.

Chapter 17

Jillian and Ben were ecstatic with the reviews they had received following the publication of the latest issue of 'All in a Day's Work'. The interviews with Maggie and the accounts of the lessons Jillian had observed had gone down very well with their readership and their Facebook page had been flooded with messages of congratulations and anecdotes about amusing spelling blunders that people had observed. Jillian's favourite was the photograph of a restaurant menu which proudly advertised its 'dick of the day', or for those who were not so hungry, its 'small dick of the day', while another eaterie in the same town was offering 'lion chops' as one of its main dishes. She had also enjoyed the post about a well-known proof-reader who was advising writers to keep her contact details close to where they 'right' and, to top it all, a local optician was promising a full 'rectal examination' with every eye test.

Now they were planning the next edition of the magazine. Ben's best friend, Joel, had stopped by the office a few days ago and had related an amusing story about his dad, Kevin, who worked as a dentist in the city.

It had given Jillian an idea. She would do an issue about teeth and all the various people who work in professions or industries connected to promoting good dental health. She had a scheduled interview with Kevin today at his own home.

Jillian liked to be punctual. She arrived at exactly the appointed time and rang the doorbell. Joel opened the door and ushered her inside where she was met by several friendly faces.

"This is my mum, Bridget," Joel began, making the necessary introductions. "And this is Sue Ellen," he added, as a little girl about two and a half years old came toddling out of the kitchen clutching a teddy bear in one hand and a biscuit in the other. "And Sue Ellen's dad, Matthew," Joel continued as the child's father appeared, trying to entice his daughter away from the newcomer before she would run her sticky fingers over what looked like a very expensive suit.

Jillian shook hands with Bridget and Matthew and tousled the little girl's hair. "Sorry," she said, "I didn't realise that you had a child in the house or I would have brought her something. She's gorgeous."

"She doesn't actually live here," Joel explained. "Matthew is my sister's boyfriend. They're just visiting for a few days." He then went on to clarify that Sue Ellen didn't live with Matthew and Georgia either but was simply enjoying a holiday with them.

"Georgia?" quizzed Jillian who was getting a bit confused about the relationships.

"Did I hear my name mentioned?" The most

stunning red-haired beauty had emerged from the front room where she had been chatting with her father. Joel introduced his sister to the journalist.

"Georgia and Matthew are staying with us for a few days," Bridget now explained. "Sue Ellen is Matthew's daughter but she lives with her mother in England. This is actually the first time we've ever met her."

"Gosh, that must have been quite emotional for you all," mused Jillian.

"You can say that again," quipped Bridget, scooping the little girl up into her arms and giving her a big kiss. "We're just hoping that Suzy and Ralph will allow this to become a regular occurrence. Now, let me take you in to meet the dentist."

Without further ado Jillian was escorted into the front room for her interview with Kevin Shaughnessy.

★★★

Imogen stood at the window marvelling at the growth of the stalks which were now standing high in the flowerbed by the front door and revelling in the fact that it was still light so far into the evening. Soon there would be a blaze of colour in those beds and they would all be planning spring and summer events. As she watched, an unfamiliar car pulled up and a young man stepped out, consulting a piece of paper in his hand and glancing at the number above the door. It must be someone looking for Bradley, she surmised, or possibly one of the other elusive tenants. But the man walked up and pressed the buzzer for their own apartment. Imogen went out to investigate.

Speaking with an English accent, the man asked for Jillian and explained that he was delivering some brochures and other documents on behalf of Kevin Shaughnessy. A blank stare from Imogen prompted clarification that Jillian had met with Kevin earlier in the day in relation to an article she was preparing on the subject of teeth and dentists.

"Of course," said Imogen, smiling now and inviting the stranger to come in. "She told me all about it."

The English guy followed her into the apartment. "Kevin had none of these brochures in the house at the time," he explained. "He promised Jillian that he'd collect some from the surgery and send them to her via Joel and Ben but I just happened to be coming in this direction anyway and offered to drop them in." He handed over the papers he was carrying.

"That's very kind of you," Imogen remarked, "though I would have expected Jillian to have given out her office address rather than this one."

The young man looked embarrassed for a moment. "I'm sorry," he said, "I hope this isn't an intrusion. It's just that she seemed keen to get started on the article right away. She left both addresses."

"No, not at all." Imogen was annoyed with herself for what must have come across as petulance and hoped that Jillian hadn't overheard. She called to her friend who was relaxing in her own room, announcing the arrival of her visitor. Then she took another look at the young man and remembered some of what Jillian had talked about an hour or so ago. "So you're the living proof that unconventional relationships can work," she mused, thinking aloud.

Jillian came in to the room at that point and glared at her friend. She then turned to her visitor and apologised for the intrusion into his privacy, assuring him that anything of a personal nature that Kevin had told him would not go beyond 'these four walls' and that she hoped she hadn't compromised her professionalism by speaking to her flat-mate. She glared at Imogen again and introduced them properly.

"Matthew, this is Imogen Tomlinson who shares the apartment here with me. Imogen, this is Matthew Mowbray who is to all intents and purposes Kevin Shaughnessy's son-in-law."

"But not really a son-in-law?"

Jillian now looked daggers at Imogen and sighed with frustration. Could she not see that this was none of her business? But Matthew didn't seem to be too concerned. He laughed and accepted Jillian's offer of coffee. She went to the kitchen to make it.

"I'm sorry," Imogen said. "Jillian will give me what for when you leave and she's quite right to be angry with me but she was telling me something about your family life while we were having dinner and how you and your ex-wife seem to have worked things out to suit everyone concerned. It's just that my boyfriend's mother is getting married this year and he's not sure how he feels about it. I come from the most conventional of families myself so I don't feel qualified to advise him. Not that there's anything he can do about it anyway. It's her decision. But I apologise for quizzing you. It just slipped out."

Matthew nodded his head. "It's OK," he affirmed. "I can't deny that I've been through some tough times and I've done some things I'm not proud of but yes, we've come out the other end and we're very happy now. I have a little girl, Sue Ellen."

"I know. Jillian said she was gorgeous."

There was a knock at the door.

"That'll be Grant now," said Imogen.

Coffee was served and Grant was introduced to Matthew. The conversation turned to more general matters about work and the weather as well as Jillian's forthcoming magazine. It was Imogen who brought it back to families. "I was telling Matthew about your mum getting married," she said to Grant. "He also has had some issues in his family over the years."

Grant looked startled for a moment. Matthew was a total stranger. Imogen should really learn when to keep things to herself. But then he sighed. What harm could it do? "My family is totally fucked up," he declared.

Both Jillian and Imogen jumped in to defend the family they had come to love and respect but Grant insisted that things had changed with his mother's recent engagement. The atmosphere in the family home was a bit weird.

"I would probably win a weird family contest over you," professed Matthew.

"I doubt it," Grant stated. "I have no father. I don't

even know who he was. Same goes for my half-sister. All we know is that it wasn't the same person. Now my mum has suddenly decided to marry my other half-sister's father. Robyn's already sixteen years old so what on earth took her so long to make up her mind! It didn't bother me when the three of us were all in the same boat but now I'm starting to resent this man. He's trying to change the whole dynamics of our family. Can you really beat that?"

"At least you don't have a sister who was almost murdered by a gang of drug dealers or an ex-wife whose brother and sister are married to each other."

This remark was met with looks of astonishment all round.

"See! I told you I would win," Matthew smirked. "It's actually a half-brother on her mother's side and a half-sister on her father's side so there's no blood relationship between them. It's all perfectly respectable. And to top it all her dad's new partner has just had a baby, well, a few months ago to be accurate. So that means that my daughter has an uncle who is younger than she is herself."

"No!"

"Yes, seriously."

They shared a few more family secrets and ended up having a good laugh. Grant admitted that he was just a bit anxious about the forthcoming change in his family circumstances and that he should really be rejoicing that his mother had found happiness. "Everything in our family has revolved around that accident that killed my uncle back in 1990," he said at last.

Imogen flinched. How strange that Grant's trauma dated from the same year that was for ever preying on her mind.

Grant was still speaking. "It'll be good to put that behind us once and for all. Even Aunt Thomasina is letting it go at last. I think she has finally accepted that we will never know who was responsible. And Alastair has made great progress in the last couple of years. He may not be the person he could have been but he's happy in himself."

"Alastair?"

"My cousin. He was badly injured in the same incident."

"Hit and run?"

"Yes."

Grant took a deep breath and then said something that made Imogen's blood run cold. Her heart seemed to stop beating for a moment. "Maybe we'll even get through the next year without dwelling on the anniversary of the event. Our house has been like a morgue on the tenth of November for as long as I can remember."

The tenth of November!

With shivers running down her spine Imogen quietly rose from her chair and went to the bathroom where she was physically sick. And then the tears came and she cried until her eyes were raw and bloodshot. How was she to face Grant again after this?

Chapter 18

Maggie was over the moon when her dad telephoned to congratulate her on the article in 'All in a Day's Work'. He so rarely showed enthusiasm for any of her achievements.

"Thanks, Dad," she said, feeling elated. "How did you even know about it?"

"Your mother put a copy of the magazine through my door."

"And you didn't just throw it out with the junk mail?"

"She left a message on my phone, telling me what was in it."

Maggie felt a warm glow of contentment. So often she had longed for praise from her dad, for a sign that he still loved her, really loved her. "Well, thanks for reading it," she said now. "I'm still looking for a proper job but those classes are tiding me over nicely in the meantime."

There was no response for a moment and then he spoke in a broken voice. "I'm sorry I haven't been a better father to you, Maggie."

Alarm bells started to ring. "Are you all right, Dad?"

"Not feeling great, to be honest."

"Lawrence and I will call round later. Can we bring you anything?"

"No, nothing. But it would be nice to see you."

Maggie ended the call. Her initial pleasure had very quickly turned to worry. She hoped that Lawrence wouldn't mind forgoing the planned trip to the cinema; her father was not exactly his favourite person but she had a feeling that something was wrong, something worse than usual.

By the time they arrived the relatively convivial attitude had vanished and Maggie's dad had reverted to form. He spoke gruffly and smelt of drink. They didn't stay long.

"What on earth did your mother ever see in him?" Lawrence sighed, as they drove away. It was a rhetorical question because he knew that Maggie was just as exasperated with the constant disappointments as he was.

"I think he's lonely," Maggie replied, trying as always to make excuses for his behaviour. On this occasion she wasn't sure whether she was relieved or upset to find that he didn't appear to be ill and vulnerable after all, just blotto.

"If he is, it's of his own making," observed Lawrence with a logic that she couldn't dispute.

"I know." Maggie nodded her head in agreement. "But he's still my dad and I keep hoping that he'll snap out of it and turn into a nicer person. And take better care of himself. Did you smell the drink on his breath?"

"Mmm. I wasn't sure whether you had noticed that."

"It would have been hard not to."

They arrived back at Maggie's flat and went inside. It was too late now for the film they had picked out so they decided to stay in and see what was on television. Lawrence scrolled through the channels and found an episode of *Grantchester*; good, they would both enjoy that. They snuggled down on the sofa with a glass of wine and some cheesy crackers.

"Sorry the evening was ruined," Maggie murmured. "I wish my family was a bit more normal, like yours."

Lawrence pulled her close. "We have our own faults too," he told her with a grimace, thinking of his sister and her unplanned pregnancy, "and the evening has not been ruined, not in the least."

Maggie gave him a grateful smile. How had she managed to find such a kind and considerate boyfriend? But somewhere in the back of her mind she was telling herself to be careful. Her mother had been madly in love with her father once. They had been blissfully happy. So what had gone wrong? How could she be sure that history wouldn't repeat itself? And how should she respond if Lawrence asked her to marry him? She was pretty sure that he was leading up to it. So many marriages were failing nowadays. But surely they were rock-solid; they loved each other; they would make it work. And after all she would be thirty in a couple of months' time; her parents had just been too young.

Chapter 19

No-one was able to lift Imogen out of the state of lethargy that descended on her after Grant's unexpected revelation. He himself had no idea that her listlessness was anything to do with the bombshell he had dropped during Matthew Mowbray's visit to the flat that evening. Imogen had eventually re-emerged from the bathroom saying that she was feeling ill and had made up a story about someone at work having the flu and how she must have caught it from him. She had persuaded Grant to go home and let her sleep it off on her own. She had used the same excuse to shun attention from Jillian and from her parents but a week had now passed and Grant was becoming suspicious.

"You would be better by now if it was the flu," he insisted, feeling her forehead and declaring that she didn't have a high temperature. "You maybe have some kind of a virus. Why don't you make an appointment with the doctor? You're definitely still not yourself."

Imogen knew that she didn't have the flu or any other kind of virus. But she had no enthusiasm for Grant's presence and couldn't even look him in the eye.

"I don't need a doctor," she whined, lashing out at the man she loved. "I just need a bit of time on my own."

Grant winced at her cruel words. She knew she had hurt him. She felt awful knowing what he had been through with Zoe. But she just couldn't sleep with him and make passionate love with him. Not now that she knew the truth. Not now that she knew it was her very own parents who had ruined his family life, who had killed his uncle and left Alastair for dead on that lonely country road. If only she had never read that diary. She would have been none the wiser. But she had read it. And there was no getting away from it. She had to make a clean break.

"Are you breaking up with me?" he asked, the heartache all too evident in both his eyes and his voice.

"Yes," Imogen replied, struggling to keep her emotions under control. "We're not right for each other."

"How can you say that?" Grant exploded with rage and bewilderment. "We're perfect together." He searched her face for clues but she turned away from him, knowing that she would so easily fall under his spell. She had to resist his charms, no matter how compelling.

"I'm sorry. I just think we've reached the end of the road."

"I don't believe you. You're bluffing."

"Why would I do that?"

"I don't know. I don't know! But you can't do this to me. Not after Zoe. I can't take it again. Please Imogen. I love you. You love me. I know you do."

Imogen didn't answer him. She loved him to

distraction and couldn't bring herself to deny it. But she had to let him go. It was over.

"Please go home now," she whispered, her heart breaking. "We're just prolonging the agony."

Grant stared at her in disbelief. Then he turned on his heel and marched out of the apartment, slamming the door behind him so hard that a glass ornament her mother had given her for Christmas toppled off the sideboard and smashed into several pieces on the hard wooden floor. How ironic that it was something that had come from Joanna. Imogen burst into tears.

★★★

Upstairs, Jillian was facing a dilemma of her own. Bradley had asked her to move in with him.

"I'd love to," she admitted, "but I can't leave Imogen in the lurch. She couldn't afford the full rent for this place on her own. We've only been here for a few months. It wouldn't be fair."

Before Bradley could answer they both heard the door slam and ran to the window. Grant was getting into his car. Without even a backwards glance he drove off like a maniac.

"They've had a row," Jillian muttered. "He'll be back with his tail between his legs before the day is out."

"I don't know about that," observed Bradley. "He looked really cross. I've never seen him like that before. But he can be moody. Maybe it's for the best. Imogen will soon meet someone else."

"You don't really like him much, do you?"

Bradley thought about the question for a moment. "I don't dislike him," he then pronounced. "It's just a bit weird spending time with him now that he's dating your best friend. I mean, I've known him for years but he never bothered with me much. Always seemed a bit aloof."

"I was kind of hoping that she would stay with Grant," Jillian mused. "They appear to be well suited and he already has his own house. I thought it was only a matter of time. And then I would have no problem moving up here with you. Does that sound selfish?"

"Selfish!" exclaimed Bradley. "It's anything but selfish. You're putting Imogen first instead of yourself. Or me. What we do or don't do shouldn't be dependent on their relationship."

Jillian realised that there was some truth in that. "Sorry," she breathed. "I love you. I do want to move up here. I'll tell her today."

"What do you think she'll do?"

"Well, this is sure to be a temporary blip with Grant so I reckon he'll entice her over to his place for some great make-up sex and maybe she'll stay. If not she can always move back in with her parents or look for someone else to share with. I'll continue to pay my half for a month or two to give her some leeway."

"But you'll be living here?"

"Yes, I'll be living here. As from today."

"Oh, Jillian, you won't regret it. I love you so much."

"I know you do. And I love you too."

She edged him towards the bedroom. "Now let's take a look at the décor in here. I might want to make a few changes."

Bradley smiled and allowed her to lead the way. They didn't come out for the next two hours.

★★★

Imogen stared at her friend in disbelief.

"You're moving out! You're leaving me here on my own! Well that just puts the icing on the cake. What a god-awful day. First Grant and now you."

Jillian waited for her friend to regain her composure. So Grant really had gone. She could have timed her announcement a bit better. "I'll only be upstairs," she reasoned at last. "We'll still see each other all the time. I'm sure Grant will be back. The two of you are perfect together."

"Grant will not be back." She almost screamed it at her. "It was me. I told him to go."

Jillian took a step back. "But why?" she stammered. "I thought the two of you were blissfully happy."

"So did I."

"Look, everyone has the odd row from time to time. I don't know what it was about but it'll blow over. Phone him up and tell him you didn't mean it."

"I did mean it. It's over."

Jillian came forward and gave her friend a hug. "I'm so sorry for making a bad day worse for you," she tried to console her. "But you must have known it was on the cards. Bradley and I want to be together. Things will work out with Grant. Just give it time."

Imogen shook herself free. "You're not listening, Jillian. I. Will. Not. Be. Getting. Back. Together. With. Grant. **Ever.** Now have you got that?"

Jillian backed off. Something serious was afoot. She was sure that Imogen would confide in her in her own time but for now she would let it go. Apologising again for her poor timing, she assured Imogen that she would not renege on her payments for a few months to give her time to find someone else to share the apartment. When Imogen replied that she wouldn't even consider living with any of her other friends or advertising for a stranger to move in, Jillian felt a pang of guilt. She would have been no different in the same situation. So what was the alternative?

"What will you do then? Try to find something cheaper? Or move back in with your parents?"

Imogen sighed with resignation. "I really don't know," she professed. "I suppose it'll have to be the cheaper option because I'm certain of one thing. I will not be moving back in with my parents. In fact I don't know whether I will ever even speak to them again."

She had managed to calm herself down. She looked at Jillian and gave her a watery smile. "Sorry," she said in a more kindly tone of voice. "Forget that I said that. I'm not thinking straight. And I'm sorry for taking my troubles out on you. You don't deserve it. I'm really made up for you. You and Bradley are made for each other and I hope you'll be very happy. You're doing the right thing."

They sat down and had a drink together. And then Imogen helped her friend to carry some of her belongings upstairs.

Chapter 20

Imogen hated herself for accepting the offer but she had allowed her parents to help with the rent so that she would not have to leave her apartment. They had insisted that she should not look for something cheaper in a less salubrious area, that they would rather pay the difference, in the short term anyway. They had even insinuated that they were happier with her having the place to herself which struck Imogen as odd at first. But when she thought about it she wasn't really so surprised. Joanna and Keith had known Jillian for years and had always been perfectly pleasant and polite to her but they had never really warmed to her or tried to get to know her family. But then Jillian's parents had been no better in that respect. However, it worked to Imogen's advantage now because Joanna started to pay much more frequent visits. If it hadn't been for the guilty secret lurking in the background, Imogen would have loved this new relationship with her mother. Sometimes Keith came along too but more often it was just the two of them chilling out for an hour or two in front of the TV, enjoying a pizza or a Chinese takeaway.

Sometimes Imogen would find herself staring at her mother, unable to fathom what must have gone on in her head over the years as she continued to conceal what she had done back in 1990. She had never considered shopping her to the police. How could she? Her own mother! It remained an unsolved mystery, an unsolved crime and, shocking as it was, nobody knew the truth but her. There was no need for her parents ever to find out that she knew anything about it. She would just push those diary entries to the back of her mind. Nor was there any need for her parents to ever find out that the boyfriend she had recently broken up with had anything to do with that family. But she missed him. She missed Grant terribly. It was so much harder to push him to the back of her mind when her body ached for him with every living breath.

Her virtual life was back in full swing. Shortly after Jillian had moved out Imogen had sent a message to her online friend:

> Hi Paulina, I'm back! Please, please, please send me something to review – something not too serious, the more mindless the better. Bring on the drivel. I've had enough of real life.

Paulina and the rest of the group of bloggers had been pleased to have her back on board and Imogen had quickly slipped into her old ways that had irritated Jillian so much. She was rarely to be seen without a phone or tablet at hand or sitting at her laptop and scribbling notes with the same old clichés about characters or settings. Her reading habits had reverted to rushing through books she had been asked to review so she had no time for others that she might have enjoyed more. Jillian had brought her several books as a present in an attempt to cheer her up; they sat on her shelf, unread.

Her phone buzzed now to tell her she had a new follower on Twitter. A quick glance at the attached profile showed her that it was yet another book blogger so she followed her back and sent a welcoming message. The more the merrier seemed to be the accepted mantra. It buzzed again. This time it was a text message:

Are you ready to talk to me yet? An explanation wouldn't go amiss.

That was colder than his usual messages. He hadn't even signed off or added a kiss. But it was churlish to complain. Their separation wasn't his fault. Imogen ignored the text. She had already told him to stop contacting her. She had apologised until she was blue in the face but she had been adamant that her decision would stand; there was no future for them as a couple. But the message unsettled her. Grant wasn't just going to let this go and why should he? They loved each other. She tried to put him from her mind and went upstairs to see Jillian. Bradley's car wasn't outside so her best friend and confidante was probably on her own. They could have a catch up.

But Jillian wasn't alone. She was having tea with her mother, Dorothy. Imogen was intrigued by the fact that Mrs Taylor-Scott was behaving in much the same way as her own mother. She hadn't visited either when the two girls were sharing the downstairs flat yet here she was now, looking very much at home. Jillian invited Imogen to join them but she didn't stay long. Unreasonable though it may have been, she felt somewhat cheated out of a proper chat with her friend. But maybe it was for the best, she told herself. Jillian would have been hounding her for answers as to why she and Grant were still estranged. If Imogen were to confide in anyone in time, it would be Jillian or maybe Holly. But she really didn't think she could speak to either of them in this instance. This was too big a secret. Her parents could end up in prison if this were to get out. She couldn't risk that. But keeping it to herself was very stressful. She wasn't sure whether the burden would just prove to be too much for her to handle alone.

Back in her own space Imogen had to admit that she was better off without Jillian chittering away in her ear about her wonderful relationship with Bradley when she herself was feeling so miserable. It was pleasantly comfortable to have the apartment to herself. It had been almost a month now. Surely the phone calls and text messages would stop soon and she would be able to get on with her life. A life without Grant. As though he had never existed. Feeling at a particularly low ebb, she started to cry. And the doorbell rang. She had almost expected it. Jillian. Apologising for the fact that her mother had been there, had stopped them having a proper talk. But it wasn't Jillian. It was Grant.

"You didn't answer my message," he said accusingly before noticing the tears streaming down her cheeks.

She couldn't just slam the door in his face. She had to let him in. But what could she say to him that would make any sense?

"You've been crying," he observed, gathering her into his arms and softening his tone.

Imogen allowed him to hold her close. It felt so good to be in his arms again, to feel his breath on her face, to smell his familiar cologne. She couldn't help herself. But the tears came even faster as she savoured the unexpected reminder of what she was throwing away. She couldn't speak.

"Are you ready to tell me what's wrong?" he urged, gently freeing her from his embrace and leading her to her own sofa. They both sat down. Imogen shook her head and wiped her face with the back of her hand, trying to pull herself together. Grant took a glance around the room, giving her time to respond. "There's something different about this place," he then uttered more to himself than to Imogen.

"Jillian's things have gone," Imogen explained. "She's living upstairs now. With Bradley."

"Oh!"

Imogen knew exactly what he was thinking before he even said it: "So here you are all on your own and there I am in my lonely house all on my own. Two places where we could be together and make love to our hearts' content. But you don't want to."

She hung her head, unable to refute what he was saying.

"I would never have asked you to move into the house I shared with Zoe but I had begun to look around for another property where I could begin afresh, where we could be together without you having to take on all the things that she had chosen. There wasn't much. We weren't together for long. I already feel closer to you than I ever did to her. Or I did. Until you dumped me without rhyme nor reason."

Imogen could hear her own heartbeat in the ensuing silence; it was like a hammer thumping hard on a block of stone. She didn't know what to say.

"I'm not leaving until you tell me what's going on," Grant said at last. "Surely you owe me that much."

"So you're just going to sit there all night?"

"If that's what it takes."

He took his coat off and threw it over a nearby chair. Then he kicked off his shoes and put his feet up on the neighbouring stool as though proving that he was in for the long haul. "Any chance of a coffee, at least?" he asked.

Imogen was glad to escape to the kitchen. She was finding it very hard to stick to her plan and not to throw in the towel and drag him off to the bedroom. She wanted him. She wanted to be with him. In every way. As she poured the coffee, she suddenly heard voices. As expected Jillian had come to apologise about her mother disrupting their chat and was of course surprised to find Grant looking very much at home on the sofa. Imogen pulled a face and nodded towards the door leaving her friend in no doubt that she and Grant had unfinished business to discuss and didn't want company. Jillian wished them both 'goodnight' and disappeared back upstairs.

They sipped their coffee. Time seemed to be

suspended. It was as though they had been cast ashore on a beautiful desert island whilst surrounded by a raging, deadly storm, with no means of escape.

Eventually Grant set his mug down and sighed. "Have you been in contact with Sam again?" he asked with an air of resignation.

"Of course not," answered Imogen. "Sam is a father now. Whether he likes it or not, he will have to settle down and learn what commitment means."

"But you're still hankering after him, aren't you? You were never really over him at all."

"That's not true," Imogen insisted. "I don't even think about Sam anymore. It's good having Holly back as a friend but we steer well clear of any discussion about what happened, more for her sake than mine."

"So you haven't seen him?"

Imogen assured him that she had not set eyes on her former boyfriend. However, she knew that she couldn't blame him for jumping to conclusions when she hadn't been able to offer a proper reason for their continued separation.

After some time Grant revealed that he had recently bumped into Joanna and Keith. "At least you hadn't badmouthed me to them," he said. "They were both very friendly toward me."

"I wouldn't dream of badmouthing you to anybody," Imogen replied.

"I was with Alastair and Aunt Thomasina. Getting them kitted out for Mum's wedding."

Imogen froze. Was this his subtle way of letting her

know that he has found her out? Had Joanna or Keith said something to give themselves away when they came face to face with Alastair? She needn't have worried. Grant didn't seem to have a care in the world on that score but went on to talk about his mother's forthcoming nuptials and to assure her that he had come to accept that it was a good development.

"I just wish you were going to be there," he added. "I could do with the moral support."

"When is the wedding?" she asked him.

"June," Grant informed her. "They're getting married on her birthday, the eleventh."

"That's handy," quipped Imogen. "You'll be able to get away with one present each year, birthday and anniversary rolled into one."

Grant laughed. "You're not the first to make that observation," he said.

They were starting to relax, to slip into their old ways. Grant dived in before the opportunity would evaporate.

"Come with me. Can I send you an invitation?"

"I'd rather not attend. We're not together anymore."

"We could be. You tell me why we're not."

She clammed up.

"Can I kiss you?"

Imogen felt a lump in her throat. "You never used to ask," she answered.

"That's because I knew I wouldn't be rejected."

She gazed at him, neither accepting nor declining the offer, all the while struggling with her conflicting emotions. And her resolve began to waver. Maybe it would be OK after all. Her parents had met Alastair and didn't seem to realise who he was. There had been no awkwardness. God, it was so callous but they really did seem to have buried their guilt. And sure it was years ago. Why should it affect her present-day relationships? Her whole body was aching for him now; the bedroom was only yards away. She leaned forward to encourage him to go ahead with that kiss. And her phone buzzed on the arm of the sofa.

"Let me check that for you," Grant said, reading her change of mood perfectly and teasing her. He picked up the phone and activated the message.

> Hi Immy. I have contacted the rest of the group to let them all know you have wasted enough time on that prat of a fucking boyfriend so welcome back, Gorgeous. Dish the dirt! And leave nothing out. Lol Paulina.

Grant was horrified. He shook his head in disbelief, then retrieved his coat and his shoes and headed for the door before Imogen had even read the message for herself. He was gone in a flash and something told her he wouldn't be hounding her with messages of love this time. Had Paulina done her a favour? Not if the bad taste in her mouth was anything to go by. She knew in her heart that she should break with Grant but this was not the way she wanted things to end between them. Without any further hesitation she deleted Paulina from her contacts list and composed a message to Grant.

I'm so so sorry. I don't even know that girl and will never communicate with her again. I still love you. Imogen x

Grant didn't reply.

Chapter 21

Jillian's parents had decided to take a spring holiday in Portugal. It was the first time they had gone away since Jillian moved out and they had asked her to help Vincent to keep an eye on things. Although he was now twenty-four, they all still considered him to be the baby of the family. Jillian phoned him when she got in from work.

"Hi Vinnie. I'm just checking that Mum and Dad got away OK."

"Yep! I left them to the airport early this afternoon. They should be arriving soon."

"You OK over there on your own?"

"Oh don't you start. I've had enough of that from Mum. As if I can't look after myself for a few days."

"So what are you having for dinner?"

"Never you mind. Mum has left enough food in the fridge to feed an army. I'll pick something later."

"You're not used to cooking for yourself."

"I'll manage."

Jillian was very fond of her brother. He was a whizz kid with cars and computers and loved nothing better than working on a DIY project with their father, Robert, but she didn't have much faith in his culinary skills.

"Come and have a meal with Bradley and me if you like," she suggested.

There was just the slightest hesitation before Vincent accepted the invitation. "OK, that'd be great. Give me an hour or so. I need to have a shower."

"No problem. See you about six."

Vincent was a plumber and very good at his job. He found most of his work through word of mouth from satisfied customers. Jillian knew he was a grown man now but he would always be her little brother. He had several friends, both male and female, but didn't seem to have found anyone special yet. Jillian sent Bradley a text to let him know about their dinner guest and set about preparing a meal. Something Italian, she thought; both Bradley and Vincent would like that.

They both arrived about the same time, just as Jillian finished setting the table.

"You don't mind Vinnie joining us?" she whispered to Bradley.

"Of course not," he assured her, "as long as it's not going to be every night."

They both valued their quality time together in the evenings.

Jillian plated up the dinner she had prepared; al dente spaghetti with big chunks of chicken breast and chorizo, served with a tomato and chilli picante sauce and parmesan cheese sprinkled on top. Then she took some garlic bread slices from the oven and set them on a board in the centre of the table. She reached for a bottle of wine but Vincent stopped her pouring any for him.

"I've to drive home," he reminded her, "and I have a job on first thing in the morning. I'll just stick to water please, or a coke if you have one."

She poured him a soft drink and they all sat down to eat. The food was delicious and both men appeared to appreciate her efforts. She was pleased. They all shared some gossip about their day at work and then moved on to holidays, instigated by a text arriving simultaneously with Jillian and Vincent, announcing the safe arrival of their parents in the Algarve. Vincent set down his knife and fork and licked his lips.

"Very nice, Sis," he pronounced. "Thanks."

"No problem," Jillian smiled.

Vincent held her gaze for a moment and then said, "Dad's been a bit funny recently."

Jillian looked alarmed. "In what way?" she asked.

"Well, he's been saying some strange things. Out of the ordinary. Like, for instance, he asked me if I'd had a happy childhood. And whether I was happy now, as an adult."

"It's not really like him to talk like that," Jillian agreed.

"I wondered whether he's worried that I might be gay," Vincent quipped. "Sometimes I find him staring at me in a weird way, as though he doesn't like what he sees."

"Well, are you?"

"It's no big deal nowadays," put in Bradley.

Jillian agreed. "Bradley's right. I must admit it never

entered my head that you might be gay but you really should put us all in the picture if it's true. Mum and Dad may be shocked at first but they'll soon come round. They both love you and that's all that matters."

Vincent shook his head. "But no, I'm not."

"Did you tell him that?"

"No. He didn't actually ask me if I was. And it mightn't be that at all. I just had the impression that it was in his mind but there was nothing specific."

"What else has he said?"

Vincent scratched his head, trying to remember. He just knew there had been several bizarre comments which had left him feeling uncomfortable.

"I hope he's not ill," Jillian suddenly said. "You know, checking that you're OK before …"

She didn't finish her sentence.

"I've wondered about that too," Vincent confided. "It freaked me out a bit."

Jillian began to stack the plates and said she would make some coffee. Her brother continued to look worried.

"It all started round about the time you moved in here," he suddenly recalled. "I don't mean in here with Bradley but when you first moved over here, when you were sharing with Imogen."

Jillian pulled a face and waited for him to elaborate.

"Do you remember that day I came over to help the two of you to hang some curtains? Well, the grilling he gave me when I got home was ridiculous. He kept talking about Imogen and asking me what she was like. I thought it was uncanny. I mean, it's not as if you'd moved in with someone he didn't know. Imogen's been your best friend for years. But when Mum came into the room he stopped talking about her. Totally. And kind of indicated to me that I shouldn't mention her either."

Jillian laughed. "Mum's probably jealous," she suggested. "Much as we're the ones with the fancy-sounding double-barrelled name, Imogen's family are actually much better off than we ever were. The two of us gave up years ago trying to get them to be friends. But I hope she's not being snobbish about it."

Jillian took the plates into the kitchen and left the two men to carry on chatting. She returned with three mugs of coffee and then had an idea. Imogen might like to join them; she had been on a downwards spiral since her break-up with Grant. The company would do her good. Vincent offered to go downstairs and ask.

Bradley and Jillian enjoyed a kiss and a cuddle while he was out of the room but he was back in a flash, closely followed by his sister's best friend.

"This is a pleasant surprise," Imogen stated with a warm smile. "Coffee would be great."

Jillian gave her a hug and quickly produced another mug whilst Bradley stared at the newcomer, suddenly overcome by the strangest sensation. Unaware that she had been the topic of conversation, and oblivious to the thoughts now running through Bradley's head, Imogen sat down with her friends, grateful for the distraction. Jillian had stopped asking her what had gone wrong in her relationship; it was clear that she wasn't ready to talk about it. They chatted instead about work. The latest issue of Jillian's magazine was focusing on garden furniture, timed to coincide with the beginning of summer. She had spent the day viewing some lovely patio sets and talking to the manufacturers and suppliers. Imogen had spent her day in local schools, speaking to two groups of teenagers, trying to promote a healthy lifestyle amongst them. One group had been very receptive and mannerly; the other had been difficult with a disruptive element that spoilt the experience for the rest and left Imogen feeling exhausted and frustrated. She felt sorry for the teachers in that school if that was what they faced on a daily basis.

"Tomorrow will be completely different," she said in conclusion. "I have private consultations all day with several very committed clients. And they're all at my own gym so I won't even have to travel around. It'll be a breeze after today."

It was Vincent who returned to the topic of family, reminding his sister that their mother's birthday was coming up in May.

"What about a party?" he proposed. "Would you come, Imogen? And maybe bring your parents? It's high time we got to the bottom of this frostiness between our families."

Imogen looked startled. Jillian filled her in on what had been discussed before she arrived. Bradley shook his head. "Not a good idea," he declared. "It's none of our business." Sometimes it takes a stranger to notice what should have been obvious all along. But he couldn't be sure. He would keep his mouth shut. But he was happy when both girls concurred and said it wouldn't be appropriate. It wasn't even a major milestone of a birthday. Dorothy would be fifty-three. No need for a big celebration. They would just organise a quiet family dinner.

Imogen went back downstairs. Vincent went home. And Jillian and Bradley went to bed.

"Thanks for being so nice to my brother," she murmured, snuggling up to him. "And for being so sensible about that party idea."

"You're nice to my family and friends too."

Jillian liked Bradley's parents. She was becoming a frequent visitor in their home and always felt at ease in their company. And she loved the way the two dogs yelped with excitement every time they saw her arriving at the door. But on this occasion her thoughts remained with her own family.

"I hope there isn't really anything wrong with Dad. You have to admit those things he said to Vince are a bit worrying. And why the sudden interest in Imogen?"

Bradley had his own thoughts on that but he kept schtoom. Instead he pulled Jillian even closer and softly kissed her as they melted into each other's curves.

Chapter 22

Maggie didn't hesitate when Lawrence did eventually propose to her on the eve of her birthday. Any doubts she had suffered were instantly dispelled as she revelled in a sensation of extreme happiness. She was going to spend the rest of her life with the man she loved. Greta took them out for a celebratory dinner and although she did invite Maggie's dad as well, they were all quite glad when he declined. Maggie felt guilty for being glad; was it any wonder the man didn't want to spend time with her? He was probably able to pick up on her negative vibes. But deep down she knew that she had nothing to feel repentant about; the situation was not her fault.

"Happy birthday, Mags," said Lawrence, holding his glass aloft.

"Yes, happy birthday, Darling," chorused Greta Redpath, "and congratulations to both of you."

They all took a sip of their Champagne and perused the menu.

"Mmm. Everything sounds lovely," Maggie remarked.

"I think I'll have the Camembert fritters to start with and then the turbot with the lime and ginger sauce."

Her mum and her fiancé were still dithering over their choices. Maggie looked up and took in the lively atmosphere of the popular restaurant. Suddenly she spotted someone she knew.

"Jillian!" she exclaimed with delight. She stood up and shared a hug with her friend before introducing her to Lawrence and Greta. "This is the girl who produces the magazine I was in," she added.

"Good to meet you, Jillian," they both told her, smiling.

"You too," Jillian answered. "This is my friend Imogen. We're just having a girlie night out."

Imogen made the connection right away. "So you're Maggie, the phonics teacher. Jillian had such fun working with you. She certainly made me think about my spelling."

Jillian was now noticing the Champagne flutes and the two balloons swaying in the air above the table to which they were attached with pink ribbons.

"It's your 30th!" she gushed. "Congratulations!"

"And also our engagement," Maggie said, extending her left hand to display her sapphire and diamond ring.

"Wow! Two celebrations in one. That's gorgeous."

Imogen added her congratulations and admired the ring.

"We're just having a quiet dinner with Mum tonight," Maggie explained. "Dad isn't very well and it was too short notice for some of Lawrence's family with having a

165

young baby in the house. We'll maybe organise a proper party later on. You'd both be very welcome."

Lawrence saw the raised eyebrows and clarified the reference to the baby. "My sister Tania has a four month old son with her partner, Sam. They're living with Mum and Dad at the moment."

Jillian glanced at Imogen with a worried expression. Imogen was momentarily taken aback but she smiled and decided to be bold. "I know Sam," she told Lawrence. "Tell him I said 'hello'."

Lawrence gave her a curious look. "So you're *that* Imogen," he said.

"He has mentioned me then?"

"Oh yes."

"I hope he and Tania are happy," she then assured him. "Anything we had is in the past."

Lawrence nodded his head. "Good," he said. "I think they're making it work. The baby is gorgeous. They both dote on him."

"Well, I hope you enjoy the rest of your evening," Jillian declared. "I'm sorry about your dad. I hope it's nothing too serious."

The two girls moved on to find their own table and to meet up with Holly. Maggie watched them go and then bombarded her fiancé with questions about his sister's boyfriend and his relationship with Jillian's friend. And with a sense of irritation and disappointment she contemplated Jillian's parting comment. Little did she realise then that her dad's excuse for declining the dinner invitation was genuine on this occasion. He really was ill, very ill.

Chapter 23

Catherine's wedding to Mark went ahead in June with an informal civic ceremony followed by a small reception for the family and just a very few special friends, including Bradley and Jillian and Robyn's boyfriend, Jack. Both Rebecca and Grant were on their own. Catherine looked stunning in a cream and lilac chiffon dress and matching fascinator and few would have believed it was her fifty-second birthday; she looked ten years younger. There was hardly a dry eye in the room after Mark's short speech:

I would just like to say a few words on behalf of my wife and myself to thank you for joining us here today and for the beautiful gifts we have received from you. I first asked Catherine to marry me seventeen years ago. As you all know she is a fiercely independent woman and she turned me down. But I knew that she loved me. There was just something about marriage that frightened her. We have been there for each other and for our daughter, Robyn, all through the ensuing years and I can't begin to describe the elation I felt when she finally said 'yes' after I proposed to her again just before last Christmas. And today our happiness is complete. I love you, Catherine and I love you, Robyn. And if Grant and Rebecca will allow me, I hope I can now be a father to you as well because I also love the two of you. It may be a bit late in the day but I really hope we can now be a proper family.

He turned towards each member of the family as he mentioned their name and finished by giving Catherine a kiss. He sat down.

Bradley squeezed Jillian's hand as the emotive speech ended. And then Grant stood up and proposed a toast to the bride and groom. Everyone joined in and took a sip of their Champagne. Grant remained on his feet. "I would like to add a few words of my own," he said.

This is a very happy day for our family. Rebecca and I have had a long talk about this and I know I am speaking for her as well when I say to you, Mark, that we will be proud to call you Dad. We are both very happy that our mother is finally going to be with the man that she loves and who loves her.

He hesitated for a moment before clearing his throat and continuing.

The last wedding I was at was my own. Thank you for coming today, Daphne and Adrian and you too, Erica. I'm happy that you are still part of my family and I assure you that you always will be. Zoe made me promise to move on and find love again and I thought I had with Imogen. I'm still not sure what happened there but I'm not going to give up. If Mark can wait for seventeen years then maybe I just have to be patient too.

Grant sat down. One more person wanted to speak. Gertrude.

There will be no more wallowing in self-pity in this family. We have all been in a perpetual state of shock since what happened to Raymond and Alastair twenty-six years ago. Then there was my own dear husband's heart attack and the beautiful young Zoe, dying so tragically in the prime of youth. But look at the lovely people who have entered our life. Bradley, for example. I'm so glad to see you here today, Son. And Jillian too. And as for Imogen, you're quite right, Grant. If you still love her, fight for her. But Mark, it's your loyalty that we're celebrating today. You could so easily have given up years ago. But you didn't. Welcome to the family and congratulations.

The whole room broke into spontaneous applause. Bradley and Jillian looked at each other.

"Do we tell Imogen about this?" Jillian asked.

"I think we have to," answered Bradley.

"Mmm, me too."

After the meal the guests mingled in the warm sunshine, chatting and taking photographs of each other with the happy couple against the stunning backdrop of the blue Atlantic Ocean and the beautiful cerulean sky. They had been lucky with the weather; magnificent as the chosen location in North Antrim was in its own right, a sunny day made it even more perfect. Alastair's paternal grandparents had travelled from New York. Although they lived so far away and rarely saw the rest of the family face to face, they did keep in touch and tried to be supportive in their own way. It had been agreed years ago that it would not be in the boy's best interests to have him hopping about from one continent to the other; he would live with his mother in Belfast.

"So Alastair's father was actually an American citizen?" Jillian remarked to Bradley. "I hadn't realised that."

"Yes, he has another whole family over there. Raymond had a brother and two sisters."

"And they have children of their own?"

"Yes. He's never met his American cousins but there are five or six in total."

"That's sad."

"Come and meet his grandparents. I'm not sure whether they'll remember me. I must have been about fourteen the last time I saw them."

Bradley took Jillian over to introduce her properly. He needn't have worried about them not remembering him. Thomasina and Gertrude had kept them well informed over the years and they immediately knew who he was.

They chatted for a few minutes, exchanging stories about life on either side of the ocean.

Grant was in conversation with Daphne and Adrian whilst Erica and Rebecca were busy taking selfies of themselves with various scenic backgrounds. Bradley didn't want to interrupt. He felt uncomfortable around Zoe's family and didn't know what to say to them. Yet he admired them for not allowing the tragedy they had suffered to define who they were. He went over to Catherine and congratulated her once again. Mark shook his hand and gave Jillian a kiss on the cheek. Gertrude walked with them to their car.

"Thanks for coming," she told them.

"It was a pleasure," they both assured her. "Thanks for inviting us."

They called in with Imogen on the way home. She was working at her computer, preparing an exercise schedule for one of her clients. She had forgotten that it was Catherine's wedding day.

"Look at you two!" she exclaimed noting Bradley's smart suit and Jillian's flowery dress and neat little clutch bag. "Where have you been?"

"Catherine's wedding," Bradley announced. "Alastair's aunt."

Imogen could hardly believe she had forgotten. 'Alastair's aunt' didn't quite conjure up the same emotion for her as 'Grant's mother' would have done and she was grateful to Bradley for describing it in that way and after all, it was because of his friendship with Alastair that he had been invited. But of course it *was* Grant's mother and she could have been there too if things had been different.

"Of course," she said now. "Come on in and tell me all about it. Have you any photos?"

Jillian scrolled through her phone and found a lovely portrait of the happy couple. She handed it to her friend.

"Very nice," Imogen agreed. "Can I look through the others?"

Jillian just nodded, knowing that she would want to see Grant. She watched as Imogen's eyes filled up.

"There weren't many people there," Jillian remarked. "It was very intimate."

"Did he have a girlfriend with him?"

"No, but Zoe's parents were there, and her sister."

"Oh, that's nice."

"There they are in the background of that one."

Imogen recognised the girl she had seen talking to Grant six months ago at the Christmas market. She had been so happy that day and her heart lurched at the memory.

Jillian waited until Imogen handed her back the phone. Then she said gently, "Grant made a short speech. He mentioned you."

Imogen looked at her, wide-eyed. "He mentioned me?"

"And so did Granny Gertrude," put in Bradley.

"What do you mean, mentioned me? What did he say?"

Jillian tried to remember the exact words and gave

her friend the gist of what had transpired. "He obviously still has feelings for you," she said in conclusion.

"I wish I could have been there," mused Imogen.

"You should have been there," Bradley told her. "Grant is a broken man without you. I don't know what's going on but he could have done with your support today."

Jillian glared at her boyfriend. "That's a bit harsh, Bradley," she exclaimed. "Imogen hasn't done anything wrong. She's the victim in all this."

"Is she though? I've developed a lot more respect for Grant in recent months."

"Now don't you two start falling out over me," Imogen said, trying to sound light-hearted. "Bradley is right. Grant has done nothing wrong. It's all my fault. But it's complicated. I never meant to hurt him and I do still love him. Very much."

"Well, we just wanted to bring you up to speed, let you know that you had not been forgotten. It's up to you to decide where you go from here. How long has it been anyway?"

"Three months. Well, four actually, three since we nearly made up and then he saw that stupid message from Paulina."

Her friends wished her goodnight and made their way upstairs. Imogen was left on her own to think about what they had told her. She could hardly believe it. Even as he celebrated his mother's marriage, and in the company of Zoe's family, he was still thinking of her. After all this time. And then her phone rang.

"I missed you so much today, Imogen," Grant told her. He sounded a little bit intoxicated.

"I'm sorry," Imogen replied. "I miss you all the time."

"Can I come over?"

"As long as you don't drive."

"I'll get a taxi."

"OK."

"See you soon."

So what about all those fine resolutions? Imogen had realised that she just couldn't do it anymore. She had to have Grant back in her life. She would make something up to explain away her intransigence and they would get their relationship back on track. No-one would ever be able to link her parents to the tragic events of the past. They obviously hadn't made the connection with Grant's family themselves and she would just forget about it. Damn those stupid diaries! She wished she had never seen them. She glanced at the clock. He would be here soon. And he'd be looking for answers. Imogen racked her brain.

I'll tell him that I met someone else and was temporarily confused about my true feelings for him. One of my clients at the gym. Or one of the teachers in a school where I was giving a talk. I can always make up a name. But he'll think I'm so fickle. He won't trust me not to do it again. How can I expect him to believe that I love him if I can fall for someone I've just met on a whim! He'll know I'm bluffing. Or maybe I could pretend that I saw him, or thought I saw him in a compromising situation with some other girl. They say that everyone has a double or two out there. I could say that I found out later that I had made a mistake;

it hadn't been him at all. But then he'll think that I don't trust him.

A taxi pulled up outside. Imogen opened the door and they fell into each other's arms. It felt so good, so right, so proper but Imogen still had no idea what she was going to say to him. Panic started to set in as she clung to him and they kissed hungrily. If she said the wrong thing now, she could lose him again, maybe for good this time. But suddenly she didn't need to say anything. Grant told her he had worked it all out. He knew what was wrong. With her heart in her mouth, Imogen sat down on the sofa with her lover next to her and prepared to hear the worst. Grant took both her hands in his and squeezed them lovingly.

"It all began that day I arrived here, just before Jillian moved out," he reminded her. "The two of you were chatting to that English bloke, Matthew, and we ended up having a stupid conversation about whose family was the most fucked up. Sorry, excuse the language, but it has dawned on me now that you took cold feet following our discussion that evening. And I can understand your reserve. You come from a perfectly normal family yourself where everybody follows the rules and you're nervous about hooking up with someone who doesn't. You're worried about bad genes."

Imogen could hardly believe what she was hearing but he had thrown her a lifeline. She just nodded and allowed him to continue.

"I have no idea who my father was, Imogen. I can't reassure you about my genes being healthy or honourable or anything else. All my mum has been able to tell me is that she got pregnant after an Easter vacation in 1986. She was twenty-one. She had gone to Scotland with a couple of girlfriends and she met this man at a party. He was apparently very charming. Drink was taken and one thing led to another. She never saw him again. She thinks his name was Cameron but she can't even be sure about that."

Imogen just stared at him. She didn't care about any of this. But how wonderful that she could latch on to Catherine's history as an explanation for her own behaviour. Grant thought that maybe she needed further convincing. He kept talking.

"By the time Rebecca was born Mum was thirty and you would expect that she might have developed a bit more sense of responsibility. But alas, she had not. Her pregnancy was once again the result of a very casual acquaintance with someone called David. She has no idea where he is today or even what his other name was. He never knew about the birth."

Imogen managed to speak at last. "It doesn't matter," she whispered. "I love you. I'm so sorry for panicking. I didn't even understand it myself but you're right. It must have been cold feet caused by some kind of subconscious concern."

"So you'll give me another chance?"

"Oh Grant, I should be the one asking you. Can we just forget all this and start again?"

He took her in his arms and gave her a very long, lingering and passionate kiss that left her in no doubt that their relationship was rekindled. Imogen closed her eyes and breathed in the delicious, manly scent of him that she remembered so well.

"I'm sorry I missed the wedding today," she said at last. "Come and tell me all about it."

Chapter 24

Bradley and Jillian got engaged in July, bringing about a flurry of activity from excited friends and relatives who all wanted to organise celebratory dinners and parties. Both sets of parents got on famously when they all met up for a meal, accompanied also by Vincent and his new girlfriend, Jane. Nigel and Ben celebrated the occasion at their respective workplaces with flowers and Champagne. And Imogen was over the moon on their behalf, albeit that she felt a little bit jealous that her friend had beaten her to it. She and Grant took the happy couple out for a meal at their favourite restaurant and bought them a beautiful set of crystal flutes. Now they were all at Gertrude's house for one of her garden parties. Gertrude was in her element. It was a beautiful balmy evening so she was able to use her summerhouse to great effect. A buffet supper was laid out there and the guests were mingling in the kitchen of the main house, the garden and the summerhouse, chatting and taking photographs. Alastair was proudly displaying some of the plants he had grown, both flowers and vegetables; now he led Bradley and Jillian to the greenhouse to admire his ripening crop of tomatoes.

As Imogen stood on the threshold of the summerhouse, a wave of happiness washed over her.

This is where Grant first kissed me. The night he told me about Zoe. The same night that we slept together for the first time.

Her body tingled as she thought about that. He still excited her just as much. Every time. She walked over to a plate of savoury snacks and popped one into her mouth, then poured herself a glass of rosé wine to wash it down. She could see Grant through the window; he was down the garden having a conversation with Robyn and Jack, his hands flying everywhere as he related some story, obviously something funny because they were all laughing. Rebecca was sitting on a bench with Mark. It was very clear from their body language that a close father/daughter bond was developing between them. Imogen smiled. Grant had told her that Rebecca was very happy with the new family structure. All she needed now was a boyfriend of her own. Imogen was pleased that Grant appeared to be enjoying himself. She sometimes got the impression that he was peeved about his grandmother paying so much attention to Bradley who wasn't even a member of the family; and here he was in the limelight yet again. Suddenly Imogen was aware of a movement behind her shoulder, a floral fragrance in her nostrils, a light breath on her neck. She swung round. It was Catherine.

"Hello Imogen," Grant's mother said to her, smiling. "I'm glad to catch you on your own for a moment."

Imogen looked around. They were indeed out of

earshot from anyone else. She returned the smile and raised her eyebrows. Catherine hesitated.

"What a beautiful night for your party," Imogen demurred, wondering why the older woman looked so nervous and giving her time to gather her thoughts.

"Yes, we've been fortunate with the weather," Catherine agreed.

"So you're happy with Bradley's choice for a wife? I know he's like an adopted son to you all."

"Very happy. Yes, indeed. Jillian is a lovely girl. Like yourself."

As she said this Catherine was gently easing the door shut so that the two of them would not be disturbed. Then she took an envelope from her pocket and thrust it furtively into Imogen's hand. "Read this later," she whispered, "when you get home."

Imogen looked up in alarm. "What is it?" she asked.

"I've been very selfish," Catherine said. "Very selfish."

"Selfish?"

"Grant has told me that he nearly lost you because of me, because of the way I have lived my life. I'm so sorry."

Imogen listened to this confession aghast, her mouth open with shock.

"That's rubbish!" she managed to say. "I love this family. You're some of the warmest, friendliest people I've ever met."

"But he told me how you were worried about the unknown. Wondering about his genes. And I don't blame you. You have such a traditional background yourself. Your parents are probably horrified."

Imogen somehow managed to stop herself from saying it aloud but she was quivering from head to toe and a voice was screaming in her head.

*I did not leave Grant for all those months because of any concern over his genes or over your behaviour. I left him because I was so ashamed of my own parents and the way they have lived **their** lives. The way they have brushed their criminal past under the carpet. I walked away from Grant because it was my very parents who killed his uncle and left his cousin brain-damaged!*

Catherine noticed that she was shaking and put a loving arm around her. Imogen tried desperately to get her emotions under control. She didn't trust herself to speak. Catherine gave a little, nervous cough to clear her throat.

"I have not been totally honest with Grant," she admitted at last. "I have always told him that I knew nothing about his biological father and he accepted that and never hassled me about it." She paused. "But I have written down a few things I do remember." She nodded towards the envelope in Imogen's hand. "There's probably enough information there to trace him if he wants to. I'm too embarrassed to talk to him directly about it."

Catherine eased the door open again and slipped out just as Gertrude arrived with some more canapés. No-one appeared to have noticed the clandestine meeting between the two. Imogen drank the rest of her wine in one gulp and then hurried into the house to slip the mysterious envelope into her handbag. Then she locked herself into the bathroom and cried for a solid ten minutes.

Damn those bloody diaries! I'm fed up with it. Lies, lies, lies and more lies. The repercussions of what happened in 1990 have created an enormous domino effect and one of these days it's all going to collapse and I'll be crushed at the bottom.

It was Grant's voice calling her that brought her back to her senses. This was Jillian's special day. She mustn't spoil it. She readjusted her make-up and opened the door and there he was, his face etched with concern.

"Are you OK?" he asked. "You've been in there for ages."

Imogen was getting used to casting things from her mind at will. She took his hand and assured him she was fine, then skipped back out into the garden to re-join the party.

★★★

"I know that Jillian and Bradley have gone official ahead of us," Grant murmured, nuzzling into her cheek as Imogen sat on her own sofa later that evening, "but you do know that I want us to be married too, don't you?"

Imogen felt a warm glow and snuggled up even closer.

"Is that what was wrong earlier on, when you spent so long in the bathroom? Was it because I haven't asked you properly yet? Maybe I've taken too much for granted."

When Imogen didn't answer him, Grant assumed that he was right. He slipped off the sofa and got down on one knee. "Imogen Tomlinson," he declared, taking hold of her hand, "I love you. Will you do me the honour of becoming my wife?"

Imogen beamed at him. "I will," she said. "Of course I will. I love you too."

They shared a kiss.

"I haven't got a ring or anything. Let's choose that together."

Imogen nodded. "I'd like that," she agreed. "Anyway, I don't want to steal Jillian's thunder. Let's wait for a while before going public. We can be privately engaged."

Grant squeezed back in beside her on the sofa. "Sounds good to me," he quipped suggestively. "I like doing things in private with you."

They both giggled.

Imogen had been trying to decide how to bring up the subject of the envelope in her handbag. The last thing she had expected was a marriage proposal. But suddenly she was engaged, even if it was just an understanding between the two of them. It felt wonderful. Hopefully Catherine's disclosure wouldn't spoil things. She decided not to delay it any longer.

"Your mum spoke to me today. In confidence." She reached into her handbag and retrieved the white envelope. "She gave me this."

"What is it?"

"She said she would be embarrassed to talk to you about it directly."

"What is it?"

"I don't know whether we should even open it."

"For God's sake, Imogen, what is it?"

"She said there was probably enough information here for you to trace your biological father, if you want to."

Grant went quite pale and stared at her.

"My biological father?"

"Yes."

"She has always maintained that she didn't know who he was."

"I know. She told me she has been very selfish in that respect. She said that you had never questioned her and she had just let it go. But she has remembered some stuff that would probably make it possible to trace him."

"And she gave this to you rather than talk to me?"

"She thinks that it was a big issue for me."

"Well, she's right about that! Sure you broke up with me for months because of it."

Imogen sighed. She wanted so much to refute that but she had no other explanation for her behaviour so she just ignored the comment. She handed the envelope to Grant.

"I don't want it!" he cried.

"Well I'm not opening it. This has to be your decision."

Grant went silent for a while. Imogen understood that he would need some time to get his head round it all. She kissed him on the cheek and squeezed his hand. Then she moved to the kitchen to give him space. She made herself a cup of coffee. She drank it slowly.

None of this would be happening if I hadn't come into Grant's life. He doesn't need this. He's been perfectly happy without this so-called father. And especially now that he has accepted Mark. I should never have let him believe that I was bothered about family matters. But I'm not giving him up. I love him. I'll go along with whatever he wants to do.

And suddenly he was calling her. "Imogen, let's do this together. Come back in here and we'll open it now."

"Are you sure? You can just throw it in the bin."

"You know that's not an option. Not when Mum has decided to spill the beans. But I do feel angry with her. She should not have lied to me. All this time!"

He ripped the envelope open and slipped out the piece of notepaper, immediately recognising his mother's handwriting. Imogen sat down beside him so that they could both read what she had written.

Dearest Grant (and Imogen),

Please forgive me for not talking to you in person but I am so embarrassed about the way you came into the world. I never wanted anything to do with the man who fathered you and still don't but I realise now that maybe you do and I should not stand in your way. His name was Cameron and he had a twin brother called Scott. I don't know their surname but the day I met them at a party was their twenty-first birthday. It was the second of April 1986 so you can work out that your father's date of birth would have been 2/4/65. There can't have been too many pairs of twins called Cameron and Scott born on that particular day. They lived in Edinburgh. Whether they were born there or not is another question. The party was held at a house owned by another man called Douglas McKendrick. If you really want to find him, my friend Patty can probably give you Mr McKendrick's current address or phone number. That's all I know. I'm sorry for keeping it from you until now. Do whatever you think fit but be aware that the man knows nothing about you and probably doesn't even remember me. But don't blame or threaten him in any way. What happened was as much my stupid fault as his.

She hadn't signed it. Grant and Imogen stared at the piece of blue notepaper, stunned.

"I could have had a father like everyone else when I was growing up," Grant said at last. "She had the information to find him all the time."

He had a fleeting image of all those football and rugby matches he had played over the years.

All those men standing around the edge of the pitch, cheering on their sons. The other boys running to their dads for a pat on the back after the final whistle. The stories friends used to tell me about camping trips, fishing expeditions, hikes in the mountains. The DIY projects they enjoyed, things they built. Especially Bradley. Bloody Bradley and his perfect life, always one step ahead of me! Because he had a dad. He had a role model. Someone who had been in his shoes. My experience of puberty and first love. All those unanswered questions because there was no-one to ask. Burying my first wife.

"He doesn't even know you exist," cautioned Imogen.

"And whose fault is that?"

"She never had a relationship with him. It was just a fling at a party. She obviously thought she was doing the right thing."

"That's no excuse. She should have given me the chance to decide."

"What are you going to do?"

Grant couldn't answer that question. He was in two minds about it. And he was far too angry to phone his mother. He would sleep on it and make his mind up in the morning.

Chapter 25

The curiosity got the better of him. Without any further communication with his mother, Grant booked a weekend trip to Edinburgh. Imogen went with him. Catherine's friend, Patty, had indeed been able to provide them with an address for Douglas McKendrick and didn't appear to have any qualms about doing so. If she knew anything about a connection to Grant's parentage, she did a good job of hiding it. They flew out on Friday night and booked into a popular tourist hotel where they had a few drinks in the bar and then went to bed.

At any other time Imogen would have savoured the bustling atmosphere of the beautiful Scottish city but she was nervous for Grant and couldn't relax. They called for a taxi as soon as breakfast was over and Grant showed the driver the address they had been given. Immediately he set off and started chatting to them about the weather and, having picked up on their Belfast accents, his own experience of trips he had taken to Northern Ireland.

"I love your part of the world," he told them. "I have

an aunt and uncle over there and a couple of cousins. I used to spend holidays with them when I was a lad."

"In Belfast?" asked Grant.

"No, further north. Up near the Giant's Causeway."

"Oh, it's beautiful up there," Imogen trilled. "There's some stunning scenery."

The taxi driver began to reminisce about fishing expeditions and boat trips he had enjoyed with his cousins and Grant was glad of the distraction. It took his mind off the reason for their journey.

A drive of almost thirty minutes led them to a large country mansion with extensive wooded grounds. Grant paid the fare and they both stepped out into the sunshine.

"This wasn't what I was expecting at all," Grant said to Imogen, taking her hand.

"It's beautiful," answered his awe-struck fiancée.

They walked up the driveway and approached the front door, not really sure how to introduce themselves. But they had made it this far; they would just say whatever came into their heads.

The door was open and a young woman was just making her way out with a large golden retriever dog.

"Hello," she said, smiling at them as she pulled on the dog's lead to restrain it from bounding up to the visitors. "Can I help you?"

"We're looking for Douglas McKendrick," said Grant.

She turned and called into the house, "Dad! There's someone here to see you," and indicated that they should go on in. "He'll be down in a moment." The girl and the dog continued on their way out into the road. Imogen and Grant stood awkwardly in the massive hallway with its dark oak panelling and paintings of hunting scenes and sombre-looking landscapes. There was a huge pair of antlers mounted on the wall facing them. They heard a door close and a man appeared on the stairs. He looked a little older than their parents, maybe about sixty, but was very sprightly and smartly though casually dressed.

"We're sorry to intrude into your home, Sir," Grant began, "but a family friend told us you might be able to help. We're trying to trace a couple of old friends and she thought you might know where to look."

Mr McKendrick frowned. "Who is this family friend?" he asked.

"Her name is Patricia Campbell. We know her as Patty."

Immediately the frown turned into a warm smile. "Any friend of Patty is welcome here," he pronounced, shaking them both by the hand. "Now come on in and tell me how I can help."

He took them into a cosy sitting-room with much brighter pictures and family photographs on the walls and offered them a drink but they assured him they had just finished breakfast. Grant made the introductions. "My name is Grant Cartwright and this is my girlfriend, Imogen Tomlinson. We know Patty through my mother, Catherine."

Mr McKendrick nodded. The names didn't seem to ring any bells.

"My mother was in your house some years ago. With Patty."

"What did you say her name was?"

"Catherine. Would it have been this same house?"

"Depends how long ago we're talking about. We moved here about ten years ago."

Grant was momentarily disappointed. So he hadn't been conceived in this lovely mansion. He didn't want to give too much away.

"It would have been before that," he said simply. Then with his heart thumping wildly he added, "The people we're looking for are twin brothers, Scott and Cameron. They celebrated their twenty-first birthday at your house."

Douglas McKendrick burst out laughing. "I remember now," he said. "Cathy from Belfast! That's certainly a blast from the past."

Grant and Imogen glanced at each other and pulled a face.

"She was the most stunning beauty, the belle of the ball. Everybody fancied her."

Grant cleared his throat. "Can you tell us where we can find the brothers now? Are they still here in Edinburgh?"

"Both of them?"

"Well …"

"I seem to remember that there was some kind of contest between the Ferguson lads that night and Cathy had offered herself up as the prize."

"The prize!"

"Yes, the prize-com-birthday present. A ten minute snogging session, I think it was."

Imogen had gone quite pale. Douglas suddenly realised that he could have been more discreet. He turned to her and apologised.

"I'm sorry, my dear, you look a bit shocked. This was during our student days. We were young and immature. We did silly things all the time."

Then he looked at Grant and something clicked. The shape of his nose, the colour of his hair, the look in his eyes …

"Oops!" he muttered, knowing now that he had slipped up big time. "It wasn't just a snogging session, was it?"

"No."

Nobody spoke. The only sound was a fly buzzing around the room. Imogen felt uncomfortable. This was so embarrassing for everyone concerned and it was all her fault that it had come out of the woodwork.

"You're not suggesting …"

"I'm not accusing your friend of anything," Grant interrupted, reading his thoughts. "My mother made it clear that whatever happened was consensual."

Mr McKendrick nodded his head.

"I've only just found out about this," Grant continued. "I'm not even sure what I want to do about it. Rushing over here was an impulsive reaction but I suppose I should meet him if you can tell me where to find him."

"Do you know which twin it was? I'm trying to remember who won that stupid contest."

"Cameron. His name is Cameron."

"Ah, you're in luck then," the older man told them.

"Scottie moved away years ago. He's in Canada if I remember correctly. But Cam still lives nearby. I still see him from time to time."

"Does he have a family?" asked Imogen.

"Yes, he's married to Lauren and they have two sons."

Grant's breathing became heavier. "So I have brothers," he stated. "Wow!"

Grant had grown up in a house full of females; he had always dreamed of having a brother.

Douglas McKendrick scratched his head and looked from one to the other. And then he came up with a potential plan of action. "Would you like me to arrange a meeting?" he volunteered. "I could invite him out for a drink tonight and we could just happen to bump into the two of you. I'll introduce you as friends of Patty's. You can then decide whether you want to take it any further."

"Just him, without his wife and family."

"Yes. He won't suspect anything. I won't say a word."

"That's really good of you. Of course he might not be free this evening."

"I'll give him a ring now."

Grant and Imogen told him where they were staying and then waited on tenterhooks whilst Douglas went into another room to find his number and make the call. They both cast eager glances in his direction as he came back in. Their new friend and confidante smiled at them.

"We'll be in the bar next door to your hotel at eight o'clock. Good luck."

***

Grant and Imogen were there at half past seven. They had spent the afternoon shopping and sightseeing and had then returned to their hotel for a chance to freshen up and have an early meal. Now there was a mix of excitement and apprehension as they sipped their drinks with an eye on the door of the bar. Every time it opened their stomachs lurched a little bit more. And then they saw him. Douglas McKendrick came in on his own and sat down a few tables away. They saw him glancing at his watch. He hadn't spotted them.

"I feel I'm being disloyal to Mum and Mark," Grant said. "I don't need this man in my life."

"It's an awkward situation," Imogen agreed. "But we're here now. You might as well get a look at him at least."

"Here he comes now."

Another man had just entered the pub and was shaking hands with Douglas. He sat down beside him.

"Let's get this over with," Grant stipulated. "Come on." He indicated to Imogen that she should join him as he walked towards the table where the two men were seated. She downed the rest of her drink and followed him. Douglas was as good as his word, feigning surprise and inviting the two young people to join them.

"Cam, these are friends of mine from Northern Ireland," he quipped, making room for them at the table. "Imogen, Grant, come and meet my old mate, Cameron Ferguson. Will you join us for a drink? I'll order a bottle of wine."

"Thanks," replied Grant, playing along. "That would be lovely. Good to see you, old chap."

And suddenly the four of them were sitting together, sipping glasses of a rather nice Chablis.

"So how do you know Doug?" Cameron was asking.

"We got to know him through our parents," Imogen replied. "They've been friends for years."

Cameron accepted Imogen's answer without question and a general conversation started up based mainly on the weather and the tourist industry. Grant was mesmerised. This man was his biological father! Why then did he not feel some connection? Some kind of bond? There was nothing. The man was perfectly polite but he was just like any other stranger. In fact his conversation was quite boring. Imogen studied his profile and smiled; there was definitely some resemblance there.

"Sorry," she said, realising that Cameron had caught her staring at him. "You seem to remind me of someone."

The man laughed. "Well I do have a twin brother," he quipped, "but unless you've been to Canada recently ..."

Douglas jumped in. "You should have seen the two of them when they were young lads. They were fiercely competitive, always trying to outdo each other." He turned to his friend. "Do you remember that birthday party at my place? You were vying over that girl."

"Scottie has never forgiven me for winning that one," Cameron replied. "It's always been a sore point with him. Cathy from Belfast. Every time he thinks he's got one over on me or brags about something I just have to remind him that I beat him in the contest for 'Cathy from Belfast'. He was so jealous. I wonder where Cathy is today. She was a real stunner and a good sport, the way she played along with our silly game."

Glances were exchanged and Grant gave Douglas a nod. Then, pretending that he had spotted another acquaintance over at the bar, the older man excused himself and left the table. Grant grabbed Imogen's hand to stop her leaving as well. He needed her support. He took a deep breath and came straight out with it.

"'Cathy from Belfast' is my mother."

Cameron became somewhat flustered. "Does Doug know that?" he asked. "Why on earth did he let me rabbit on like that? I'm sorry, I didn't mean any disrespect."

"I was born exactly nine months after that party."

"God!"

"I'm not here to cause any trouble. I just wanted to meet you."

The man's face was ashen. Imogen felt sorry for him. What a bombshell! The sounds of the bar took over; the clink of glasses, animated voices chatting and laughing, music playing in the background. But there was silence at their table. Douglas came back over and sat down. Cameron glared at him.

"Thanks a bunch," he mouthed.

"Would you have preferred that he came to your home and told you in front of Lauren?"

"No."

"Will you tell her?"

"Probably. We don't do secrets. It's not as if I cheated on her. I didn't even know Lauren in those days."

"Quite right," Douglas agreed. "Secrets poison a marriage."

Imogen flinched. She was still holding on to a very big secret of her own.

"At least you don't need to bother with DNA tests or anything. I can see the resemblance quite clearly," commented Douglas.

"We can if you want to," Grant offered.

"No need," said Cameron. "I'm not disputing it. But I'm going to need some time to get my head round this. Can we leave it for tonight and maybe meet up again tomorrow?"

"Yes, OK, we can stay for another day."

They arranged to meet at the same time in the same place on Sunday evening. Then Grant and Imogen went back to their hotel next door and went straight to their room. It had been a stressful evening but it could have been worse. The guy hadn't attempted to deny his involvement. And he appeared to be perfectly respectable. Things would hopefully seem better after a warm, soapy bath and an early night.

But Grant lay awake for a long time. As he stared at the ceiling of their hotel room with wide-open eyes he had another vision of those football matches from his boyhood.

My mum was always there for me and she was far more supportive than a lot of the other boys' dads put together. She made sure that I didn't miss out on any major opportunities, often by making sacrifices herself in terms of both time and money. She organised all those extra activities for me; classes in carpentry, photography, car maintenance. Would I have been any better off with this stranger in my life? I didn't feel any connection at all tonight. But let's see what tomorrow brings. He was obviously in a state of shock. Once he has had time to think about it …

Chapter 26

Jillian and Dorothy had started to plan the wedding. Bradley watched bemused as they flicked through one magazine after another, picking up ideas for the big day. He wasn't that bothered about the event himself; he just wanted Jillian to be his wife. But he wouldn't spoil it for her. If she wanted a big lavish do, he would go along with it and play his part. Vincent and Jane were in the kitchen, making toasties. Robert was making his way through the Sunday papers, engaging Bradley in conversation about the various articles that caught his attention. When he came across a feature on Portugal he was in his element, reminiscing on his visit there in the spring. He pointed to the photos of the beautiful, sandy beaches with their huge, red cliffs and the hibiscus trees with their bright orange and yellow flowers.

"There were some of those in the garden of our hotel," he told Bradley. "Apparently they bloom all year round. There were some bright red ones as well."

"They are beautiful." Bradley agreed.

"You should have seen the wild flowers too, just growing along the roadside."

"Would you go back?"

"Definitely. You should consider it for your honeymoon."

"We're thinking of a tour around Europe so you never know."

Bradley recalled that it was while Dorothy and Robert were away on that Portuguese holiday that he had first noticed Vincent's little mannerisms that were so like Imogen's. Coupled with the fact that Vincent had alluded to strange looks and comments from his dad, Bradley had grown suspicious. There was definitely some history between the two families that neither girl seemed to be aware of. But he had never voiced his concerns on the matter; it was none of his business.

Jane came in and started passing round the toasties. Vincent followed with a pot of coffee. They all stopped what they were doing and enjoyed the informal lunch. Jillian's phone rang just as they were finishing, the caller display telling her that it was Imogen. She went out into the hallway to talk to her friend but the others couldn't help overhearing her end of the conversation anyway.

"Edinburgh? What are you doing there?"

"His dad? Gosh, I thought he didn't know anything about him."

"Catherine told you?"

"He has brothers! Wow!"

"Tonight? Well good luck with that."

"Yes, OK. I still have my key so that won't be a problem. I'm over here at Mum and Dad's but I'll do it as soon as I get home. See you tomorrow. Bye."

Bradley looked up at her as she came back into the room. "What was that all about?" he asked.

"Grant has discovered his real father," Jillian revealed, "complete with a wife and two sons."

"Gosh, how romantic," quipped Jane.

"That must come as a bit of a shock," added Vincent.

Robert and Dorothy just exchanged awkward glances. Then Robert got up and left the room. Dorothy started to busy herself, gathering up the empty plates and mugs. Bradley surveyed the scene with bamboozlement and scratched his head. What on earth was going on?

The wedding preparations were put aside and Jillian beckoned to Bradley that they should go. Imogen had asked her to call into the flat and check her appointments diary. She was staying in Scotland for another night so would miss a couple of meetings she had planned for the morning. She had asked Jillian to cancel them for her and she would rearrange them later. They headed out the back door just in time to see Robert slashing relentlessly at a sturdy tree branch for all he was worth. He had abandoned the papers and, in the space of five minutes, had changed into his gardening clothes.

Jillian laughed. "What has that tree done to deserve this?" she asked her dad.

"Just felt like a bit of physical exercise," he answered her as he took another swipe at the branch. "Too much sitting around isn't good for you."

Dorothy was now scrubbing the kitchen floor so she seemed to be in agreement with this philosophy.

"Well, we're off now to get a bit of exercise ourselves,"

Jillian called to them both. "We're going to pick up the dogs and take them for a walk. I'll give you a call during the week."

They got into Bradley's car and waved to Vincent and Jane who were now at the front window.

"Your parents can be weird at times," Bradley remarked as they drove away from the gate.

"They did change tack there, very suddenly," Jillian admitted.

"Just after your phone-call from Imogen."

"What's that got to do with it?"

"Nothing," replied Bradley, "nothing at all. I'm just saying…"

He didn't really know what he was just saying. So he said nothing more. But he was more convinced than ever that there was some sort of connection. And it wasn't just with Robert. Dorothy seemed to be in on it too.

★★★

Bruno bounded out onto the gravel path and shook himself vigorously, obviously glad to be out in the open air after the thirty minute car journey. Even with the air conditioning at full blast it had been a bit stuffy in the confined space available for such a large dog. The tan-coloured boxer immediately recognised his surroundings and wagged his white-tipped tail with excitement as Bradley reached in and attached a lead to Jasper's collar before releasing him from the vehicle. They had come in the white Kia Sportage belonging to Bradley's parents.

"Why are you putting a lead on Jasper but not on Bruno?" Jillian asked, a puzzled look on her face. She was used to both dogs being restrained when they walked them.

"Bruno will be fine here in the forest park," Bradley told her. "He only wears a lead when we're out on the roads in busy traffic. He needs to get a good run from time to time to keep him in good shape."

"Are you not afraid of him running away?"

"He's too fond of his home comforts," laughed Bradley. "He would never stray too far."

"But what about him attacking a child or something?" Jillian quizzed. She had always been a bit wary of dogs herself, had never had one of her own.

"Bruno would never do that," Bradley assured her. "He's been with the family since he was a puppy, which is seven years now. He's well trained." He then turned and spoke to the pedigree dog himself, patting him affectionately on the head as he did so. "Isn't that right, Bruno? You're a good boy."

Jasper was now out of the car as well. Bradley held his lead firmly in his hand as he locked the vehicle and they all headed down the path towards the river walk.

"So Jasper isn't so trustworthy?" Jillian probed, glancing at the smaller of the two animals. He was a tan colour with black and white patches and different coloured ears, one black and one white. "What breed is he anyway?"

"He's a mongrel," Bradley explained, "a cross between a beagle and a spaniel we think. He's a bit hyper and unpredictable. And he's only about one and a half; he has a lot to learn."

"They seem to get on well together," Jillian observed.

"Definitely."

They had now arrived at the river bank. Bruno scurried in and out of the bushes sniffing at the ground but, just like Bradley had said, he came back obediently when called to heel by a brief whistle. Jillian was impressed. Strolling along and breathing in the fresh summer air, they admired the sights, sounds and scents of nature that surrounded them. A family of chaffinches were singing their hearts out high up in the branches of the beech trees to their left whilst a pair of swans sailed majestically towards them on their right hand side. A red admiral butterfly flitted past and landed on the bright pink petals of a wild rose, growing amongst the ferns and brambles. They chatted animatedly about their wedding plans and also touched on the strange behaviour displayed by Jillian's parents earlier in the day as well as the news that Imogen had relayed to them concerning Grant's sudden discovery of a father. That was certainly a turn-up for the books.

"I think I'll let Jasper off the lead for a few minutes now that we're well away from the car park," Bradley proposed after a while. "Hopefully he has picked up how to behave from watching Bruno." He leaned down and detached the blue leather strap from his collar. Jasper rolled over hoping for a tickle and then started running excitedly, relishing the freedom as he wove through their legs and around the nearby tree trunks. As soon as Bradley gave a whistle, he came back to his master, copying Bruno's example. So far, so good. Jillian and Bradley sat down on an old wooden bench facing the river.

"I don't want to be away from home too long," Jillian reminded Bradley. "I promised Imogen that I would make some phone calls for her."

"I know," Bradley agreed. "We'll just take a few more minutes. The dogs love it here." He watched as a middle-aged couple approached them with a Great Dane; this would be a good test for Jasper. As expected the little dog gave a series of excited yelps and ran over to the newcomer, sniffing with interest. But then, as Bradley and Jillian exchanged pleasantries with the older couple, Jasper returned to his playful games with Bruno and allowed the other dog to move on. He had passed the test and would be rewarded with a few more minutes of freedom. Jillian's thoughts returned to her friends and the bolt from the blue that had taken them to Scotland.

"I hope things don't get awkward for Grant. When you consider all that he's been through without any support from this so-called father, the man has a bit of a nerve showing up now."

"I suppose we can't judge him until we hear all the circumstances," Bradley cautioned.

Jillian gave him a warm smile. "I'm really glad that the two of you are getting on so well now," she enthused. "It means a lot to me with Imogen being my best friend."

"We're certainly closer now than we ever were as children," Bradley conceded. "I used to think he resented me. In fact I'm sure he resented me and saw me as an outsider, an intruder."

"He was just a child. We all make mistakes," Jillian soothed. "I think it's wonderful the way you have kept up your friendship with Alastair. People with special needs are so often marginalised in society."

"I used to love going to his school," Bradley ventured. "There was such a happy, positive atmosphere even though most of the children had serious difficulties. Some of them were in wheelchairs. Some had problems with their sight or their hearing. Almost everyone I came across had an issue with speech and language. But I never heard anyone complaining. I came away from there every time feeling so thankful for my own good health and so ashamed of the petty squabbles and grumbles that I came across so often in my own school."

"Is that why I never hear you whingeing about trivial things?" Jillian was holding his hand and gave it a loving squeeze.

"I have my moments," Bradley grimaced. "I'm not claiming to be a saint."

"You're perfect for me." She smiled into his lovely blue eyes. "I love you."

"I love you too." They shared a kiss. "Now let's round up those dogs and get back to the car."

Bradley whistled and both dogs bounded over obediently. But Jasper was reluctant to be restrained again after the unexpected freedom. He refused to stand still as Bradley attempted to re-attach the lead. And suddenly they all saw a rabbit hopping along the grass and into the bushes. The temptation was too much for the small dog and he set off in hot pursuit. Bradley whistled again but Jasper just ignored him this time.

"I'll have to go after him," Bradley muttered. "You take Bruno and I'll meet you back at the car." He handed Jillian the keys and a spare lead that he always carried. Bruno allowed her to clip it in place and walked alongside her as they retraced their steps, while Bradley headed into the wooded scrubland. There was no sign of Jasper.

I can't arrive home without him. Mum'll kill me. She loves that wee dog to bits.

Bradley's parents had acquired Jasper from a rescue centre and had nursed him back to health, not knowing whether the injuries he suffered had been caused through ill-treatment or some sort of accident. But he was part of the family now and fully recovered, displaying no signs of his former trauma. With his bright, inquisitive eyes, glossy coat and boundless energy, he was Lena's favourite.

"Jasper!"

No response.

Bradley called his name again and whistled for him but all he could hear in reply was the continuous birdsong in the branches high above his head. He ran this way and that, frantically scouring the landscape and then suddenly became aware of a rustling sound behind him. Turning round he caught sight of the little mongrel, running towards him and panting.

"Gotcha!" Bradley exclaimed as he darted forwards and tripped over the trunk of a fallen tree, landing in a pile of thistles. His hand brushed against the dog's collar but failed to grab hold of it before the animal ran off again, evidently believing that this was all part of the game. Frustrated, Bradley scrambled to his feet and brushed himself down with his hands. Then he noticed that he had scratched one hand quite badly and had just rubbed the blood which was oozing from it onto his expensive white and green striped shirt. The other hand had been covered with mud which was now smeared all over his favourite jeans.

"Fuck!" he grunted to himself and then yelled it aloud as he realised there was badger poo all over his tan suede shoes. "Fuck! Fuck! Fuck! That bloody dog!"

Jasper had vanished again but Bradley could hear his excited yelps in the distance. He tried to follow the sound but it echoed around him in all directions and he had no idea whether he was going the right way or not. He was also aware of a louder, gruffer bark from another dog so Jasper had obviously found a friend. Bradley made his way back to the path and sat down. Surely the dog would soon tire of his games and come crawling back. Several minutes passed and at last he glanced to his left and there he was, approaching the bench. But the drama wasn't over yet. As Bradley jumped up and reached out to attach the lead, Jasper started running round in circles, sidestepping him every time. With a final lunge forward Bradley slipped on a patch of slime and ended up knee-deep in the river, only just managing to steady himself and avoid falling over completely. His clothes and his shoes were ruined.

Jillian stared dumbstruck as Bradley eventually

arrived back in the car park, trailing a much subdued dog who seemed to have realised at last that he had been very naughty. Bradley was soaked from the thigh down, his feet squelching in muddy water which was still seeping from his shoes, his shirt covered in blood and slime, his hair sporting pieces of twig and bramble.

"Don't ask!" he fumed. "I am never taking this dog out again!"

"You can't get into the car like that," declared Jillian. "You'll ruin the upholstery."

"I don't care," he snorted irritably. "It isn't my car and it isn't my bloody dog!"

"Is your sports bag still in the boot?"

"Oh, you're right. Thank God for that!"

And it was. He had been to the gym with his dad earlier in the week and kept forgetting to bring his kit home. Thankfully he stripped out of the wet trousers and footwear and put on the shorts, socks and trainers from his bag. They were a bit damp and sweaty from his training session but a great deal better than what he had taken off. They looked ridiculous with his stained shirt so he took that off too, changing into his tee-shirt. Jasper was a bit dirty too but he had survived his adventure relatively unscathed. They all clambered back into the car and headed home. Bradley was still bristling with rage. Jillian struggled to keep a straight face, knowing that her fiancé too would see the funny side of it later. She didn't dare ask what had happened to the rabbit.

★★★

Imogen thanked her friend for sorting out her appointments. She was in the bar again with Grant, waiting for Cameron Ferguson to turn up.

"It was no trouble," Jillian told her. "I assured them both that you would be in touch ASAP and that you'd been unavoidably detained in Scotland."

"I hate letting people down at the last minute."

"They were fine about it. Honestly. Don't give it another thought. You've enough on your plate with all that is happening over there."

"Grant is really nervous. I wish this guy would hurry up and get here."

"I'm sure he is. Wish him good luck from me." Jillian paused for a moment and then remembered something. "By the way," she said out of the blue, shocking Imogen to the core, "do you realise that you still have some of your mum's diaries? I noticed them when I was looking for your appointments book."

"You shouldn't have been anywhere near those!" Imogen snapped.

Jillian was surprised at the almost violent reaction and immediately backtracked. "Sorry," she said. "I opened the wrong drawer by mistake."

"I hope you didn't start reading them."

"Of course not. Why would I?"

"Well why did you even mention them?"

"I don't know. I just remember you telling me about something your mum had written and seeing them there rang a bell. Did you ever solve the mystery?"

"No. Yes. I don't want to talk about it."

"You're very touchy all of a sudden. Maybe I should have had a wee read. I could go back in tonight."

Imogen felt the panic rising. "Leave them alone," she hissed. "Those diaries are private."

"I'm joking, Imogen! I won't go near them. I'm only winding you up."

"Promise me you won't."

"Yes, OK. I promise. Cross my heart and all that."

The door opened and Cameron walked in followed by several other people.

"He's here. I have to go. Talk to you tomorrow." Imogen disconnected the call and put her phone into her pocket.

Grant stood up and shook Cameron by the hand. He smiled a welcome to the surrounding group but nobody smiled back. Cameron introduced them.

"This is my wife, Lauren, and these are my boys, James and Henry." The two boys were only teenagers, about twelve and fifteen. "I've told them who you are."

Lauren shook his hand rather stiffly. The two boys looked like a couple of fish out of water. They just stared at him with a glazed expression.

Cameron then ushered the other man forward.

"And this is Hunter McLeod," he announced, "my solicitor."

Grant took a step back. "Your solicitor?" he queried, pulling a face.

"Yes," Cameron stated looking a little shame-faced. "He's just going to keep me right. After all we don't know yet what you actually want from us."

Grant had a momentary vision of the happy home he had shared all his life with his mother and sisters and the stabilising influence of Mark on the whole family since he had married Catherine just over a month ago. He didn't need this man who obviously had no real interest in him. He suddenly felt angry.

"Well, I'm sure your solicitor will have a hefty bill for you for wasting his time on a Sunday," Grant retorted, beckoning to Imogen that she should follow him as he made his way towards the door. "If that's your attitude, then I don't want anything from you. A civil friendship was all I expected but that's obviously out of the question."

Imogen was still reeling from her phone-call with Jillian but she was nonetheless able to appreciate that Grant had made the right decision in walking away from these people.

"I've never been so proud of you," she gushed, as they walked out into the street.

He squeezed her hand, grateful for the support.

"Half of my genetic make-up comes from that bastard," he ventured to say.

"Never mind, you must have got the good half. I love you. And I love your family, your real family back home."

"Did you see his wife? I've never seen such a sour face in my life." He consulted his watch. "Let's go home, Sweetheart. I'll see if we can get an earlier flight."

Grant managed to get them booked on the first plane out in the morning so they cancelled breakfast, settled their bill and went to bed. It would be an early start. And then suddenly Grant saw the funny side of the situation and started to laugh.

"I suppose maybe he did have a point," he said to Imogen. "How did he know I wasn't a gold-digger? I never even thought of taking money from him."

"That's because you're not a mercenary person," she replied. "It's one of the things I love about you."

"Maybe he's a millionaire."

"Who cares? I didn't like him."

"He didn't seem so bad yesterday but I didn't like him today either."

"I think it's the wife. She's got her clutches into him and told him to be careful."

"You're probably right. Anyway, on another note, what has Jillian done to upset you? You were giving her a right good rollicking before they arrived."

Imogen clammed up.

"Go on, tell me what she's done."

"She just invaded my private space, that's all."

"But you asked her to. She was doing you a favour."

"She didn't need to go poking around the whole flat."

"You're very prickly all of a sudden. Is there something in particular that you didn't want her to see?"

"Maybe."

"Sounds intriguing. Would I be allowed to see it?"

Imogen didn't answer that. She just explained it away as tiredness and stress and promised that she'd apologise to Jillian for getting so rattled about nothing. But deep down she was worried about the diary issue. Could she really go through life with the knowledge of what she had discovered there always lurking in her subconscious? If she was going to stick with Grant she had to. There was no other way.

Chapter 27

Imogen rearranged her appointments as soon as she arrived home and apologised to her clients for cancelling at such short notice. Grant headed into the store. He had some students arriving for work experience and he wanted to be there to supervise so that he would be able to give their teachers an accurate report. Imogen stayed at the flat. She completed some paperwork and then waited nervously for Jillian to arrive home. She would have to apologise for her outburst; as Grant had pointed out, the girl had only been doing her a favour. She heard her car pull up and opened the door.

"Coffee?" she suggested.

"As long as I'm allowed over the threshold."

"Oh, don't be like that. I'm sorry. It's been a stressful few days."

Jillian came in and slumped down on the sofa. "OK, apology accepted. How did it go with Grant's dad?"

Imogen filled her in on the evening's events, as she made the coffee.

"He must be so disappointed," Jillian surmised. "What

a dreadful reception to have got. The guy could have made some effort to get to know his own son. Money matters should have been well down the line."

"Well, Grant wants nothing more to do with him. But I'm glad we went. He would always have wondered what he was missing."

"Not much by the sound of it."

"Anyway, I'm sorry for being so sharp on the phone," Imogen now said. "I have been meaning to return those diaries to Mum but I need to do it furtively because I slipped one out without her knowing one day. I'd rather she didn't know that. You wouldn't come with me by any chance, and distract her while I slip it back in?"

Jillian laughed. "Would she really mind that much?"

"Please?"

"Yes, of course I'll come if you're really serious. Do you want to do it later this evening? Bradley's working late tonight. I'll tell you all about our adventures with his dogs on the way over."

"That'd be great. Sounds intriguing. Let's say about seven-thirty."

★★★

Imogen let herself into the family home and breathed a sigh of relief. There was no-one in. She was still chuckling at Jillian's description of a very wet and bedraggled Bradley and his seething reaction when Jillian had eventually enquired as to the fate of the rabbit.

"Make yourself at home," she said to her friend, picking

up the post and wondering where her parents had gone. They had obviously been out all day. She set down the books she was carrying on the hall table and checked to see whether any of the letters were addressed to her. Although she had now been living in her own flat for the best part of a year, there were often items still delivered to her at her old address, usually unimportant fliers from companies where she had bought something or reminders about dental appointments and suchlike. She hadn't bothered to inform everyone of her new address. Today there was a glossy white envelope which looked interesting. She took it into the lounge and carefully opened it.

"Gosh," she said to Jillian. "It's an invitation to Jenny Bosworth's wedding. I haven't even seen her for at least a year."

Both girls had been friendly with Jenny at school.

"Oh, I forgot to tell you," Jillian replied. "I met Jenny a couple weeks ago and we had lunch together. It was just after Bradley and I got engaged. She told me about her wedding coming up soon and said she was going to invite us. Mine has probably arrived today too."

"Wow! She must be having a big do if we're on the list. We were never really that close, not recently anyway. I don't know how she can be bothered with all that palaver."

"You never were the fairy princess type," laughed Jillian.

"Always been a bit of a gamine," Imogen admitted. "I sometimes wonder how you and I became such good friends. We're quite different in some ways."

"Nothing wrong with that," Jillian declared. "I like people who know their own mind and don't always just follow the crowd."

They started to reminisce about their schooldays, guessing who else might have been invited and laughing about some of their exploits from days gone by. It would be fun to see everyone again. And Jenny had included a 'Plus One' invitation so Imogen was pleased that she'd be able to bring Grant along too. They had both completely forgotten the reason for their visit to the house until suddenly they heard the front door opening and Joanna appeared in the room with her three diaries under her arm. Imogen turned a ghastly shade of pale.

"Hi girls. Thanks for returning these at last," Joanna said.

She turned the books over in her hand and suddenly she also turned a funny colour and looked accusingly at her daughter.

"I don't remember lending you this one," she declared. "In fact, I know I definitely didn't."

Imogen bit her lip. Jillian glanced from mother to daughter in total bewilderment. Keith came in and asked what was going on; you could have cut the atmosphere with a knife.

"Where did you get it?" demanded Joanna.

"I took it from the wardrobe myself," Imogen admitted.

Keith looked at the date on the front of the book and glared at his wife. "I told you to destroy those stupid diaries," he shouted. "It's bad enough that you kept them but to start lending them out for her to read …"

Imogen interrupted him. "It was you who gave me the first one, Dad," she reminded him. "You brought it over to the flat and told me to take good care of it."

"But not this one!" he screamed.

"It's OK," Joanna hissed in his ear. "I tore out the pages." Although she tried to keep her voice down, her comment was still audible to the girls.

There was no going back now. Imogen realised that the story was going to come out. And suddenly she saw red.

"I have been protecting you," she shouted at both parents. "You may have tried to remove the evidence but I know what happened that day and you should both be ashamed of yourselves instead of trying to blame me."

Joanna gulped and then glanced at Jillian. "And presumably you know what happened too then. You must have told her."

"Hey, leave me out of this," Jillian retorted. "I shouldn't be here at all in the middle of a family dispute. I'm feeling very uncomfortable witnessing this row."

"Sorry," Imogen mouthed in the direction of her friend and then faced her mother again, looking for an explanation.

"How could Jillian possibly have told me anything?" she asked. "This has nothing to do with her. We didn't even know each other in those days. I was three!"

"You went to playschool together."

"What?" the two girls chorused together.

Imogen would quiz them later about why they had never revealed this information before but for now she feared that they were getting off the point.

"I didn't want to have this discussion," she said more calmly. "I came here tonight to replace your diaries and I would never have mentioned them again. But you have intercepted me and you have to admit that in doing that you have put me in a very awkward position. You can't just brush something so serious under the carpet. You should have come clean at the time."

"Don't be so melodramatic, Imogen. It's not that big a deal. We were in a bad way about it for some time but we did eventually manage to put it behind us and move on. It's history now."

"We hoped you would never find out about this," added Keith.

Imogen shook her head. "This is outrageous," she said vehemently. "How can you say it wasn't a big deal? You left a little boy to grow up without his father!"

Keith and Joanna exchanged shocked glances.

"As if the brain damage wasn't bad enough on its own!"

"He has brain damage? I thought he was perfectly healthy. How come you've never mentioned that before?"

They both looked at Jillian, as though they expected a response from her.

Jillian picked up her bag. "I'll see you back at the flat," she told Imogen. "I've no idea what's going on here but I do know it's got nothing to do with me and I'm finding this extremely embarrassing." She walked towards the door.

Joanna blocked her way. "Your parents are just as guilty as us," she told Jillian. "We were all in this together."

This was news to Imogen. It was even more shocking than she had imagined. "And not one of you thought of going to the police?" she asked, albeit rhetorically because she already knew the answer.

Keith nearly exploded with rage. "Get a grip, Imogen," he said sharply. "What the hell did it have to do with the police? It was a totally private matter."

"My parents are guilty of what?" Jillian asked, starting to shiver with foreboding despite the warm summer evening.

They all stared at each other and paused for breath. Imogen was confused; something wasn't adding up here.

"You can hardly call it a private matter when somebody died," she uttered at last, bursting into tears.

Joanna looked her straight in the eye. "What do you mean, somebody died?" she now asked her clearly distraught daughter. "Who died?"

Imogen tried to compose herself. She wiped the tears away with the back of her hand and spoke as calmly as she could.

"Look, I know it must have been an accident but you were surely aware of the consequences. I had no idea that Jillian's parents were there as well. It's all starting to make sense now; the way you've never been that enthusiastic about our friendship. You didn't want them reminding you about what happened and neither did they so you've just kept away from each other."

"Well that's true enough," Joanna admitted. "We could hardly believe it when the two of you became such good friends about eight years later."

"Will someone please tell me what this is all about," Jillian pleaded.

"Alastair," replied Imogen, wiping more tears from her cheeks.

"I thought his name was Vincent," said Keith.

Joanna suddenly understood. She was shocked to the core.

"Alastair!" she shrieked, the blood rushing to her head. "Grant's cousin, Alastair! You think that your father and I were involved in that hit-and-run accident that killed that boy's father! Have you taken leave of your senses? How could you believe such a thing of us, Imogen?"

"Well you give me another explanation!" cried her equally distressed daughter. "You may have torn out the pages but you left enough clues. I know that you did it. Have you no shame?"

Joanna grabbed Keith's hand and dragged him with her as she stormed out of the room. Imogen and Jillian heard them go upstairs together. There were raised voices as doors were opened and closed and then suddenly it went quiet. Both girls were now so bewildered that neither of them spoke. Joanna came back down alone.

"I never wanted you to see this or know about it," she announced, "but I cannot have you thinking that I killed someone."

She handed Imogen an envelope.

"These are the four missing pages from my diary. Your father is even more mortified than I am that you are going to read them but he agrees with me that we have no other option."

She left the room.

Jillian was now quivering from head to toe. She had been thrust into the middle of God knows what and was very confused. Imogen put an arm around her.

"I'm so sorry, Jillian," she said with sincerity. "I really don't know what we're going to discover here. But let's find out."

She opened the envelope and took out the pages. She could see at once from the distinctive logo that was used throughout that they had indeed been torn from the diary she had read. She looked at the first one.

Looking forward to a nice relaxing evening. Imogen has been safely deposited with Mum and Dad and they are over the moon about having her all night. Dot and Robbie have also arranged for their little girl to be looked after overnight so we can let our hair down and have some fun. They'll be here soon and I think I have everything under control. The dinner is in the oven, the table is set and the drinks are on ice. Bliss!

Not at all what she was expecting! Imogen made sure that Jillian had also finished reading it before she turned it over to find out what had happened on the second missing day. Dot and Robbie? Presumably that was Dorothy and Robert. How strange that they had never owned up to knowing one another in the past when they had actually visited each other's homes for dinner parties.

Why keep that secret? Especially when the two girls had become such good friends. Jillian indicated that she was ready to move on and Imogen turned the page.

I cannot believe what happened last night. There is just no excuse for it. Robbie told me that he had seen Keith and Dot snogging in the kitchen. I didn't believe him so I took a look and there they were, bold as brass. I was so shocked. It was either order her from my house or get my own back by doing the same with Robbie. And he was pretty sexy. So I kissed Robbie and I made sure that Keith saw us. We had all had far too much to drink and one thing led to another. Before I knew it he had his hand down my blouse and I was fumbling with his zip. We ended up having sex. The more I heard Dot moaning with pleasure as my husband fucked her, the more I allowed hers to screw me. It was like a game and I was determined to win it. Maybe I did but it doesn't feel that way now.

Imogen froze. This couldn't be true. Not her mum and dad. And with Jillian's parents! It was too disgusting for words. Jillian almost fainted. She started to cry.

"There are two more pages," Imogen blurted out. "Do you want to see them?"

Jillian couldn't even bring herself to speak. She just nodded.

What on earth have we done? I feel so dirty and ashamed. I cannot even look at Keith and he is talking about divorce. But he started it! Our marriage is probably over. This wasn't just sex. It was debauchery. It was sordid and base and lewd and the awful thing is that we both loved it at the time. But where was the common sense and the decency? I was blinded by jealousy and flattered by Robbie's compliments. What a mess.

The girls just hugged each other and said nothing. There was nothing to say, nothing to take away the hurt they both felt. There was one more page.

We have organised a new playschool placement for Imogen. Hopefully we will never see those people again. We are both so sorry. We are going to try to make it work. We do love each other. But Keith is sleeping in the spare room and I don't see that changing any time soon. Talk about regrets!

"What has all this got to do with Alastair and the accident?" Jillian asked, still totally baffled about the events of the evening.

"Nothing, as it turns out," mused Imogen, "nothing at all."

"So that bit about a little boy and his father... I remember you reading it out to me, months ago."

Joanna came back into the room and overheard this remark.

"That was your brother, Vincent, that I was worried about," she said.

"Vince? How come?"

"I was concerned at first that Robbie might not be his father, that it might actually be Keith."

Both girls gasped. Could this get any worse!

"But you got that sorted?"

"Well, I never heard anything to the contrary so I presumed everything was OK in that respect."

Jillian thought about it for a moment and tried to work out the maths. "This all happened in November 1990, isn't that right?" She had taken note of the dates on the diary pages. "Vince was born on the fourteenth of August 1991."

"I know. I remember seeing them that autumn," recalled Joanna. "I was out jogging in the park and they passed me with a baby in a pram. It did give me a shock because the timing definitely appeared to make it a possibility."

"Where's Dad?" asked Imogen.

"He's upstairs," her mother told her. "He's too embarrassed about it all to come down and face you."

"I'm sorry for thinking you were a murderer."

Mother and daughter exchanged a sad look and shared a hug. And then they both hugged Jillian. She was wondering about how to broach this with her own parents. And she was very concerned about her brother's date-of-birth.

"Can we go home now?" she said, weary beyond words.

"Yes, let's go," agreed Imogen. "I can't wait to get back home to see Grant."

Chapter 28

Imogen was floating on cloud nine. So her mum and dad had cheated on each other, once, a long time ago. What did it really matter? They had forgiven each other in time. They had stayed together and not ruined her childhood by splitting up or even making her aware of any animosity. They had accepted Jillian as her friend and had always been polite and welcoming towards her even if they had avoided any contact with her parents. And they had had nothing whatsoever to do with the accident that had devastated Grant's family. It just happened to be the same day in history. Coincidences happen all the time.

A week had now passed since her mother's revelations and Grant was amazed that Imogen had taken it all so well. They were upstairs in Bradley's apartment, all having a Friday night drink together. He had the windows wide open to let the warm summer air filter through. Jillian, who was preparing some nibbles in the kitchen, had been true to her word in that she had promised Imogen not to reveal her original suspicions about the diary entries.

No-one else ever needed to know that she had got it so wrong. Grant was telling Bradley all about his experiences in Edinburgh.

"The guy sounds like a real tosser," Bradley declared. "You're better off without him."

"Without a doubt," agreed Imogen.

Grant smiled at her. "You are so level-headed and sensible," he told her. "I can't get over the way you've been so light-hearted all week after finding out about your own parents. It actually makes what my mum did seem quite tame in comparison; at least she wasn't married."

Imogen sighed. If only he knew how much worse it could have been. She was just so happy that her fears and suspicions were unfounded in the end. Disgusting as her parents' behaviour had been, it was still the lesser of two evils in her mind.

Jillian came in and set down some crisps and crackers. "I'm still very shocked about it all," she admitted. They had both been quite open with the boys about the facts of the case. "It really is quite dreadful to think of them behaving like that. Imagine if the four of us suddenly did a swap and started to play about with each other's partner, and all under the one roof."

"And the language Mum used to describe it!" said Imogen. "I didn't think she even knew words like that."

They all giggled.

"Well all's well that ends well," Grant professed.

"Is it though?" exclaimed Bradley who could contain himself no longer. "Have none of you noticed that Vincent is the image of Imogen?"

The other three stared at him and went quiet.

"I wouldn't stir things up, if I were you, Mate," Grant advised after a moment. "The girls are feeling more fragile than they are letting on."

"Mum said she had worried about Vince at first but that it had turned out to be OK," Imogen recalled hesitantly.

Jillian was less certain. "I don't think that is what she said," she argued. "She indicated that she had assumed everything was OK because she had never heard otherwise."

"What age is Vince?" Bradley asked Jillian.

"He'll be twenty-five later this month. Technically it is possible. I've already worked that out. But surely they would have told him long ago if…"

"Sorry girls, but there's quite a striking resemblance. I noticed it weeks ago. This diary you have discovered just confirms what was already going through my head. It all makes a lot of sense to me now."

"So you're saying that Vince is only a half-brother to me?"

"And also a half-brother to me!" Imogen added.

"It's definitely looking that way."

"Let's not do anything rash," Grant advised, thinking of his own recent experience. "I think we've all had enough drama for this week."

The conversation changed to work-related issues when Jillian suddenly heard a beep on her phone and commented that it was a message from Maggie, the teacher who had got her so interested in linguistic phonics back in December. She never had got round to booking a place on an evening course herself but hadn't ruled it out. Maggie was reminding her that the enrolment date was coming up very soon if she was still interested in doing something creative or artistic. She also apologised for not contacting her sooner or organising the party she had suggested, explaining that she had been preoccupied with family matters on account of the fact that her father had taken ill.

"It's nice the way clients keep in touch with you long after their own edition has hit the shelves," remarked Imogen. "I remember meeting Maggie that night at the restaurant. Didn't she say something then about her father being ill? That's why he wasn't there."

She also remembered that Maggie's fiancé was a brother of the girl who now had a baby with Sam. She smiled to herself. She felt no animosity whatsoever and hoped that he was happy.

"I've made lots of friends through the magazine," Jillian agreed. "I like Maggie. I also heard from Kevin the dentist this week. He had got wind of my engagement and sent us a lovely card."

Grant remembered meeting the English guy, Matthew Mowbray, who had delivered some items to the flat on Kevin's behalf. That was the day he had voiced his concerns over family issues, the day when Imogen had suddenly taken ill and had ended up breaking with him. Which was quite ironic now when he thought about it; her own family was just as bad as his! He smiled to himself. He had liked Matthew.

"Actually, I might be seeing Kevin and his family again quite soon," Jillian now revealed. "My next issue is going to focus on the hospitality business up north and Kevin's daughter, Georgia, has been able to put me in touch with some people who might have an interesting slant on things. First of all there's someone called Annabel Popplestone who apparently runs a very popular B & B and then there's someone called Susan Matthews who recently opened a tea-room and gift shop with her husband Derrick. I'm looking forward to meeting them all. They're related in some way to Georgia's partner, Matthew, through his ex-wife."

"That all sounds very civilised," said Bradley.

"Yes," Jillian concurred. "I love to hear about couples who manage to move on after a split and don't show any animosity." Then she laughed, thinking of what Bradley had noticed about Vince. It couldn't be true. Could it?

Grant was now talking about his latest promotion in the store with barbecues and garden furniture selling like hot cakes. "We can hardly keep up with the demand for burger baps and sausages," he remarked.

At the mention of barbecues Bradley revealed that he had spent the day fitting new locks and alarms at a large house which had recently been burgled while the family were all out in the back garden enjoying the good weather and cooking steaks and kebabs on a barbecue. Opportunistic thieves had slipped in through a side door and had made off with several items of worth.

Their conversation was interrupted by a phone ringing. Grant picked his up and saw his mother's name highlighted in the caller display. "Hi Mum," he said pleasantly.

He heard her breathing heavily before she spoke. "I can't believe that you went to Edinburgh without even telling me," she then blurted out in an accusatory tone.

"Well what did you expect me to do?" he responded, frustrated at her attitude. "Why give me that information if you didn't want me to act on it?"

"I just thought you might have kept me informed."

"Like the way you kept me informed for the past twenty-eight years!" Grant retorted.

"I suppose I deserve that," Catherine acknowledged.

"How did you know anyway?"

Grant moved away from the others, out into the hallway at the top of the stairs. There was no need to subject everyone to his mother's wrath. She was obviously feeling quite rattled.

"I had a call from Douglas McKendrick," Catherine then told him. "He had got my number from Patty."

"Yes, I met him," Grant admitted. "I liked him."

"And apparently you met Cameron."

"Yes, and I didn't like him."

"Douglas said he has two young sons."

"That's right," said Grant. "I met them too and they couldn't crack a smile between them."

"Will you be seeing them again?"

"Absolutely not." He was aware of a sharp intake of breath at the other end of the line and decided to put his mother's mind at ease, once and for all. "You have no need to worry, Mum," he said more kindly. "Just for the record, I think that you did the right thing in never contacting him about me. It's not as if you were ever in a relationship with him. You were tricked into playing a silly game before you were really mature enough to understand the consequences. You didn't need him in your life and neither do I. I have a dad. His name is Mark and I'm very happy with him because I know that he loves you." He could hear his mum starting to cry. "Just forget about Cameron," Grant advised her, "but thank you for telling me about him. I'm sure it wasn't easy for you." He paused. "And there's something else I want to thank you for. Thank you for keeping me when you found out you were pregnant. You could have given me away or even had me aborted." He looked up and saw Imogen coming towards him. "And then I would never have had the chance to live my life and fall in love with my beautiful fiancée."

"Fiancée?" Catherine repeated through her tears.

"Yes, it's not official yet but we will most certainly be getting married very soon."

Imogen put her arms round him as he ended the call and then they sat down together on the top step and kissed.

"That was lovely," Imogen breathed. "I overheard most of what you said." She thought about it for a moment and then asked him whether he believed that Vincent was in the same boat if Bradley's suspicions did indeed turn out to be true.

Grant considered her question carefully before answering. "Every case is different," he then said. "I would have reacted differently if Cameron Ferguson had been more welcoming. In a way I feel quite gutted but I'm not going to dwell on it or let that waste of space define who I am. But yes, somebody needs to put Vincent in the picture. He deserves to know the truth."

"I think Jillian will have to tackle her mum and dad about it."

"Well, you'll all have my support, whatever you decide to do."

"I love you."

They kissed again. "I love you too," he said. "Let's go for a walk."

Calling good-bye to their friends they skipped down the stairs and out into the evening sun.

Chapter 29

Robert was mowing the lawn when Jillian arrived on Saturday afternoon. She had decided to come alone and was not at all sure what she was going to say even though she had gone over and over it in her mind. She chatted to her dad for a minute or two and then headed into the kitchen, where Dorothy was baking some scones. The first batch were already out of the oven and resting on a cooling rack. They smelt delicious.

"Take one while they're warm," Dorothy said as she watched her daughter eyeing them greedily. "You'll get butter and jam in the fridge."

Jillian lifted one and took a bite. Mmm, there was nothing to beat her mum's baking. She remembered coming home from school when she was a little girl, tired and hungry, often soaking wet from the walk in the rain. She would deposit her schoolbag on the hall floor, drape her wet coat over the back of a chair and relax in front of the fire with a drink of juice and a freshly baked biscuit or scone. In the summer the snack would be taken in the garden. But the yeasty, mouth-watering aromas would still be wafting around the house. Just like today.

"So what brings you here on a Saturday?" Dorothy asked her. "Is Bradley not with you?"

"No, we'll do something together later on, maybe take the dogs to the beach," she said, as she spread some butter on the rest of her scone. Then she chuckled to herself, wondering whether they would give Jasper another chance at freedom or keep him firmly attached to the lead. Bradley's shoes had been beyond repair after last week's incident but they had at least managed to get the stains out of his shirt and his jeans. "He's helping his dad with some DIY stuff this morning, re-grouting the shower cubicle, I think."

"Good for him. You've definitely got a top bloke there. Seems he can turn his hand to all sorts of things."

"I'm glad you like him. It's important to me to have love and respect within the family."

"You sound very serious all of a sudden. Is everything all right?"

"I don't know."

Dorothy looked alarmed. She wiped the flour from her hands and removed her apron. "Is it the wedding?" she asked. "I know that the stress of organising a wedding can be overwhelming."

Jillian reassured her it was nothing like that and that she and Bradley were fine.

"Well what is it then?"

She took a deep breath. "I was wondering about Vince," she then said. This was so difficult but she had to ask.

"What about Vincent?" probed her mother.

"Is he really my brother, my full brother?"

Dorothy instinctively knew that Jillian had found out something. That question wouldn't just have come out of the blue. She hesitated. Jillian could see a vein pulsating in her neck.

"So he might not be?" She took her mother's silence to be some kind of confirmation.

"Spit it out, Jillian," Dorothy said at last. "What exactly do you know?"

"I know what happened between you and Keith Tomlinson," she answered, "and I know that Vince was born nine months later."

Dorothy sat down and put her head in her hands. So this dreadful act had come back to haunt her after all, even though so many years had passed. She closed her eyes and bit her lip. What could she say? Talking to her own daughter about this was so embarrassing.

Jillian was still speaking. "And I know about Dad and Joanna Tomlinson."

Dorothy gasped.

"At least no baby resulted from their liaison," Jillian stated with a hint of sarcasm.

"It only happened the once," her mother argued hopelessly. "Your father and I were still in a healthy relationship at the same time."

"So you're saying it could have been either of them."

"I suppose so, yes."

"But you did have the necessary tests done, to find out?"

"Well …"

"It's just that some people have noticed a resemblance between Vince and Imogen."

"I know but …"

Robert came in and immediately noticed his wife's distressed state. He had overheard Jillian's last remark. "What's going on?" he thundered.

"She's asking about Vincent," Dorothy explained in a pained voice. "She knows."

"I'm not sure that I do," Jillian quibbled. "Will one of you please give me a direct answer. Who is Vincent's father?"

They both stared at her, then at each other.

"Who on earth has been blabbing?" Robert exclaimed. "Could they not let sleeping dogs lie?"

"We've only just found out ourselves," Dorothy added. "There was always a chance that he was Keith's but we didn't want to think about it. We just put it from our minds and carried on regardless. But recently we noticed something in his expression, something that reminded us of Imogen. So we did the tests."

"Twenty-five years too late!"

"Yes."

"Does he know?"

"No. It was easy to get his DNA. We just borrowed his toothbrush and a tumbler he had used. He didn't suspect a thing."

"And when exactly were you going to give him this life-changing information?"

"Jillian, don't be so hard on us. We have been trying

to decide on the best course of action. It's very stressful for us too."

"Does Keith Tomlinson know about this?" asked Robert.

Jillian nodded her head. "He does now, since Monday night. That is, he knows that your night of debauchery is common knowledge. But how could he possibly know the result of any test you have done at this late stage? He is still assuming that you would have done that years ago and that you must have tested positive as far as a match with Vincent goes because you never told him otherwise."

They all turned their heads as Vincent and Jane marched up the driveway, giggling and laughing, as though they didn't have a care in the world.

"Keep out of this, Jillian," Robert hissed. "We will tell him ourselves when the time is right."

Jillian just shook her head. Would the time ever be right for such an announcement? But then suddenly she saw it from her dad's point of view and she felt sorry for him. He must be devastated. No wonder he had appeared to be so angry recently, like that time he attacked the tree in the back garden. She placed her hand on his arm and gave him a watery smile. Then she turned to her brother and his girlfriend.

"Hi, you two," she called over to them. "How are things?"

She went outside to chat to them, giving her parents time to compose themselves.

"Can you keep a secret?" Jane asked her, still giggling.

"A secret?"

Vincent blurted it out before she could either agree or decline. "We're going to have a baby."

Jillian was dumbstruck. She jostled them away from the house, further down the garden and sat down on the wooden bench under the cherry tree. Jane sat down beside her.

"You're really pregnant?" she said to Jane.

Jane nodded her head. She had the happiest look on her face and was bubbling over with excitement.

"You haven't been together for very long," Jillian cautioned. "Are you sure it's a good idea?"

"Hey, we're banking on your support," Vincent cut in. "It's already happened so we're determined to be positive about it. It's too late to deliberate on whether it would be a good idea or not."

"And when are you planning to tell Mum and Dad?"

"Soon. But not just yet so keep it to yourself."

Jillian sighed. So she had to keep one secret from him and another one for him. Life was becoming a bit complicated.

"What about your own parents?" she asked Jane. "Do they know?"

Jane stopped smiling and pulled a face. "Not yet," she admitted. "I'm not looking forward to that conversation."

"So what are your plans? I mean, where are you going to live when the baby arrives?"

"We're going to start looking for a flat and move in together as soon as possible," Vincent revealed.

"You're the first person we've told," Jane announced.

"Well then let me be the first to congratulate you both," she said, giving Jane a hug, "but I can scarcely believe it. My baby brother starting a family before me!"

"I'm not a baby," Vincent countered. "I'm almost twenty-five."

"Shh," whispered Jillian, "here comes Mum."

Robert had calmly resumed his gardening. Dorothy had put the final batch of scones into the oven and was now offering to make coffee. Life carried on as though nothing had happened.

Chapter 30

Jillian's mind was in a whirl of confusion. She was trying to keep too many secrets for too many people and she just wanted everything out in the open so that they could all get on with their lives. She kissed Bradley good-bye as he left for the gym early on Sunday afternoon and looked out of the window to check that Grant's car was still away. She had noticed him driving off alone some time earlier. Good, there was no sign of it; so Imogen would be downstairs alone. She went down and rapped on the door.

"I think we need a heart-to-heart about what is going on with our parents," Jillian told her friend.

"I'm not sure that I can ever face mine again," Imogen agreed. "It's almost a week since that awful night. I'm absolutely mortified that I accused them of killing someone and covering it up. As if they would ever do something like that."

"But at least you found out that it wasn't true."

"I know. I've been up and down all week. One minute I'm over the moon that I was wrong about it and the next

I'm feeling awful for ever believing it in the first place."

"The fault is theirs, Imogen, not yours. You shouldn't be beating yourself up about it."

"Thanks, but that's easier said than done."

"I found out something yesterday," Jillian now revealed tentatively.

Imogen looked at her questioningly.

"Bradley was right. Vincent is only a half-brother to me. Your dad is his biological father."

"Oh my God, what a nightmare! Are you sure?"

"Yes."

Jillian explained how her parents had avoided the truth for years until they recently found it staring them in the face, how they had eventually checked it out just a few weeks ago.

"And here's another titbit of information for you. Your brother and mine is now expecting a baby with a girl he has only known for a matter of weeks. He's afraid to tell Mum and Dad."

Another gasp from Imogen. "What on earth are we going to do about all this?"

"Well," said Jillian, "I've had an idea. They were best friends once upon a time. If we can just get them together again …"

★★★

Keith and Joanna arrived first.

"We're meeting our daughter and her boyfriend," Keith told the maître d' as they handed over their coats.

"They said the table would be booked in the name of Cartwright."

"Yes, of course. This way, please," said the young man, consulting his clipboard and then ushering them towards a fairly private area in the far corner of the restaurant. "Can I bring you some drinks while you are waiting?"

Keith ordered a beer and Joanna chose a glass of Prosecco. They surveyed their surroundings and both commented on the friendly ambience of Imogen's chosen venue. Joanna liked the soft lighting and the pastel shades used for the furnishings and the napery. Keith loved the appetising aromas coming from the open kitchen. They were glad that Imogen and Grant had invited them to join them here for a meal. It would be a chance to clear the air between them. They liked Grant. They were still horrified that Imogen had believed them capable of some form of manslaughter and humiliated that they had been forced to reveal what had really happened on the night of the accident that had claimed the life of Grant's uncle but they were desperate to put the trauma behind them and get back on an even keel with their daughter. Joanna fervently wished that she had never mentioned the fact that she had kept diaries in her youth. But what was done was done and she couldn't change it. She just hoped that Imogen would allow them all to draw a line under it and that tonight would lead to them all making a fresh start.

Their drinks arrived and they started to relax and peruse the menu. It was ten minutes or so before they saw another couple approaching their table.

"Here they come now," said Joanna, standing up to

greet her daughter. She hadn't actually seen her face to face since that dreadful evening when all had been revealed and relationships had been decidedly icy so she was feeling quite apprehensive. She braced herself for a showdown.

But it wasn't Imogen. It was Dorothy Taylor-Scott, accompanied by her husband, Robert. Joanna recognised them at once but the newcomers seemed to be momentarily confused.

"We are meeting our daughter and her fiancé," Joanna heard Dorothy tell the maître d. "They told us the table would be booked in the name of their friend's grandmother, Gertrude Cartwright, and that she would also be joining us."

The maître d' glanced at Joanna who indicated that she would sort out the problem.

"Hello, Dot," she then said amicably to her old friend. "I think our young people must have thrown us together on purpose."

"Joanna!"

Keith and Robert had now recognised each other as well. They shook hands awkwardly and sat down. A waiter arrived to take a drinks order for the new arrivals.

Joanna realised now that the table which was set for six, as they had expected, was actually joined to another larger table with place settings for an extra six people. At first she had just thought that another group would be in quite close proximity to them.

"You haven't changed at all," Joanna said to Dorothy. "I knew you at once."

Dorothy was very much on edge and shifted nervously in her seat.

"I saw you once," Joanna continued. "I was jogging in the park and you passed me, both of you. It was shortly after your little boy was born. You were pushing a pram with a blue quilt so I knew you had had a boy."

Dorothy's eyes filled with tears. "Did Jillian tell you?" she asked.

"Tell me what?"

"About Vincent."

Keith was listening in. "He's mine, isn't he?"

Dorothy bit her lip and nodded.

"Only in a biological sense," Robert put in.

Keith rejected this remark with an angry scowl. "You had no right keeping that from me, no matter how it came about," he snapped.

The two men eyeballed each other, sparring for a fight.

"It could just as easily have been Robert and me," Joanna reminded her husband, her face flushed crimson with embarrassment.

"Would we have been so secretive about it?"

"Who knows? Maybe we would."

"I'm so sorry," Dorothy said. "He was my little boy no matter who had fathered him. I wanted to believe he was Robert's and just put the other possibility from my mind. But he's not. We only found out a few weeks ago."

"And the girls know?"

"I presume that's why they have arranged this meeting. We thought we were just having dinner with

Jillian and Bradley along with Bradley's friend Alastair and his grandmother."

"We were just expecting Imogen and Grant along with Grant's cousin and their grandmother."

Suddenly the ice was broken and they were all laughing. The two women embraced.

"I've missed you over the years," Dorothy whispered.

"Me too," admitted Joanna. "We could have been such good friends."

Even Keith and Robert managed a wry smile as they acknowledged that the past had caught up with them and they may as well try to make the best of it. They heard footsteps and voices behind them and turned to see the maître d' approaching with another six people.

★★★

Imogen was delighted that her plan seemed to be working. She had deliberately staggered the arrivals at the restaurant to give the parents some time on their own before they would join them. Now she was elated to see that her mother and Jillian's mother were actually hugging. She introduced Grant to Jillian's parents and Jillian introduced Bradley to hers. Then Grant introduced his cousin, Alastair and their grandmother, Gertrude, adding that Alastair was one of Bradley's best friends. Imogen had included Alastair and Gertrude in the party mainly as a distraction; by booking the table in Gertrude's name, she had hoped that no-one would smell a rat. And it had worked. The only thing was that there were still two empty seats at the far end. Vincent must have taken cold feet. He and Jane had been due to turn up about ten minutes prior to their own arrival.

Well, at least one secret was out in the open. But Vincent still had to be told. And only the two girls knew about Jane's pregnancy. Apart from that things were going remarkably well and they all enjoyed their meal. There was an awkward moment just as they were finishing their desserts when Joanna alluded to her diaries and mentioned her horrified reaction on discovering that her daughter had believed she was a cold-blooded killer. Imogen glared at her and Jillian vigorously shook her head in an attempt to silence her but the damage was done. Grant stared at Imogen, looking for an explanation. She bit her lip.

"What is your mother talking about?" he asked.

"Nothing, it doesn't matter. Just a misunderstanding."

Joanna still didn't realise that Imogen was desperate to keep this from her boyfriend.

"It wasn't 'nothing' when you came storming into my house accusing me of all sorts. Hit and run accidents; brain damage; dead fathers etc. etc."

Gertrude gasped. Alastair looked upset. Grant almost burst a blood vessel. And Imogen burst into tears. Too late, Joanna made the connection. But in a strange way it led to a new camaraderie between Keith and Robert when they both realised that they too had been implicated in the imaginary plot. Even Gertrude ended up laughing and told Joanna to stop apologising. Grant took a little longer to forgive.

"You made me feel guilty about my unconventional family structure, when in fact you believed that your own parents had killed my uncle," he slated her. But he kept his voice down lest Alastair should get the wrong end of the stick. For once they were all quite pleased that he was slow to understand what was going on and Bradley, supportive as ever, had deliberately engaged his friend in a conversation about football to protect him from any insensitive remarks.

"Only after you begged me to come back to you," Imogen reminded him. "I did try to let you go even though it was breaking my heart. We were apart for months."

"Thank God it wasn't true. That's all I can say."

"Hear! Hear!" chorused several voices and Grant gave her a hug.

Robert, Dorothy and Jillian had all tried phoning and texting Vincent throughout the evening but to no avail and their two seats remained empty. Jillian was not totally surprised. When she had mentioned the proposed meal she had got the impression that they were not yet ready to go public with their news and were possibly worried that she would blurt it out. But now suddenly all three of their phones buzzed at once and they all read the same message:

Trying to contact someone who knows the owner of this phone. He's had an accident.

Chapter 31

They heard it on the news on their way to the hospital. There had been a gas explosion at a site where Vincent had been working. There were several injuries and at least one fatality. All they could do was hope that he was alive and would pull through.

Robert was distraught. First he had discovered that Vincent was not his biological son; now the boy he loved could be dying or already dead. Whoever had sent the text message could not give them any more details. Robert had immediately taken charge. He had asked Bradley to take Dorothy and Jillian home and despite their pleas to the contrary Bradley had followed his wishes. Robert had promised to get in touch as soon as he had any news. Gertrude and Alastair had been despatched home in a taxi. Grant went with Imogen and Joanna.

Keith and Robert now sat side by side in the small waiting room in the hospital ward, each lost in their own thoughts. It was Robert who had suggested they should both go together.

"This is weird," Keith said at last. "I don't even know the boy. He won't want me here."

Robert responded by scowling and stating the obvious. "He's your son."

"But I was never there for him. Not a single birthday present over the years. No family Christmases. Nothing."

"He's had a good life."

"But not with me!"

Robert let out a big sigh. "I didn't know, Keith, I didn't know," he insisted. "But even if I had known, what would you have had me do? Leave Dorothy and expect you to leave Joanna. Abandon our two girls to grow up without fathers."

"Of course not," Keith snapped. "I don't know what you should have done."

There was a flurry of activity in the corridor outside and they knew that other relatives were waiting in other similar rooms nearby. They felt numb. This was no time for arguments and recriminations.

"I only have myself to blame for what happened that night," Keith now stated. "I started it."

"But I took it all up a level."

Keith grunted. "That's certainly true," he agreed. "It was only a kiss at first. I wouldn't have dared take it any further until you did."

"You shouldn't have been kissing my wife!"

"I know. I'm sorry. It all started so innocently."

Almost twenty-six years had passed but the details of that night were still engrained on his memory.

"We were in the kitchen and I was pouring her a

drink. We were both a bit tipsy. Dot commented that the glass I had given her was chipped at the base and I said something about that not being a major issue as that part of the glass would be nowhere near her pretty lips. So she pouted her lips at me and we giggled. It was just a mild flirtation. Then she started teasing me about other plates and cups that were sitting in the dish rack in front of us and pointing out that several of the items there also had little chips or cracks. She picked up a white coffee cup with a thin red stripe – I can still see it in my mind's eye – and ran her finger along the rim. Then she took my hand and ran my finger along it to show me that it was a bit rough. Her touch was very sensuous. 'I could cut my lips on this,' she suggested, 'and then you'd have to kiss them better.'"

"Sounds like Dorothy, all right. Just a bit of playful banter."

"Yes, but she pouted those ruby red lips at me again and I couldn't stop myself giving her a kiss. And that's when you saw us."

"And we all know what happened next."

They stopped reminiscing and tried to focus on the present.

"I want to be part of his life, Robbie. If he still has one."

"Understood."

"And I don't want Joanna left out in the cold. We were all in this together."

"That won't be a problem."

Why had no-one come yet to explain what was

happening? They heard more voices outside, someone crying, another family being ushered into a side-room.

"You were right to send the others home," Keith remarked. "This is no place for the women or for our young people."

Suddenly the door opened and a doctor in a white coat came in and sat down. He had a very serious look on his face. A police officer followed him in.

"Which one of you is Vincent Taylor-Scott's father?" the doctor asked, looking from one to the other.

"We both are," Robert said without flinching. "It's complicated."

"We are dealing with a very difficult situation here," the policeman now told them, accepting Robert's answer without batting an eyelid. "We have three young men who were not carrying any identification. We believe that they are two plumbers and an electrician who were all working on the site. Your son's phone was found beside them."

"Are they …?" He couldn't say it.

"One of them has passed away," the doctor said gently. "The other two are unconscious."

Within minutes Keith and Robert were being escorted into another room where the body of a young man was lying on a bed, covered with a sheet. They braced themselves for the worst. As the doctor revealed the lad's lifeless face, Robert burst into tears and shivered uncontrollably. Keith was gripped with a sensation of hopelessness as a barrage of lost opportunities flashed through his mind.

So this is the son I never knew I had. And now it's too late.

Too late to tell him I always wanted a son. Too late to take him fishing and hill-walking. Too late to buy him all those missed birthday presents.

But through a haze of confusion and overcharged emotion he suddenly heard Robert's voice ring out. "It's not him. That's not Vincent. I'm sorry, I can't help it, but my tears are for some other poor father who is not going to be so lucky."

The doctor replaced the sheet and led the two men back to the waiting room where they were given some strong, sweet tea to help relieve the shock and stress they were suffering. No-one was as yet able to give them any information about the condition of the other two lads involved in the incident except to say that they were undergoing emergency surgery and that, in both cases, the outcome was still touch and go. The first twenty-four hours would apparently be crucial.

★★★

The twenty-four hour deadline had now passed and Vincent was still alive. A second lad had died during the night but thankfully Robert and Keith had not had to endure the horror of another identification; they had already been reunited with their son before it happened. The other two families had been and gone in a haze of horrendous weeping and grief. It was now very quiet in the small room where Vincent lay, still in a coma. He wasn't out of the woods yet. Various members of the family were taking turns to sit with him.

Jillian and Imogen had just taken over from their parents when they were aware of other voices outside. The nurses were being very strict about a maximum of two visitors at a time and they were constantly coming in themselves to check the equipment that was attached to Vincent's young body. Jillian looked up at the small window to see who had arrived and spotted a woman she didn't recognise. She went out into the corridor.

"You must be Jillian," the woman said pleasantly. "I'm Marcia, Jane's mother. Jane has just gone into the bathroom. She's taking this very badly. I know she hasn't been with your brother for very long but she's very fond of him. She couldn't understand why he didn't turn up on Friday night when they were supposed to be going out or why he wasn't answering his phone and then we got a call from your mother this morning. She's been quite sick since she heard about the accident, hasn't stopped crying."

"I'm sorry you had to wait so long for news of what had happened," Jillian told her, "but there was a lot of confusion about who was who, and about who was alive or dead."

"The nurse told us he's still in a coma."

"Yes, but he's stable. We're hoping for the best."

Jane emerged from the toilet and saw Jillian talking to her mum. As she burst into tears anew, Jillian could see that her face was red and strained, streaked and blotchy.

"Have you told her?" Jillian asked Jane gently in a quiet voice, nodding in Marcia's direction.

Jane shook her head.

"Told me what?" her mother asked, glancing from one to the other.

"Jane's pregnant," Jillian whispered. "That's the father of her baby lying in there in a coma. She was going to tell you soon but I think it's important for you to know right away in the circumstances. She's going to need a lot of support from you and her dad."

Marcia was speechless for a moment but then threw her arms around her daughter and held her tight. "Oh, Jane, darling, why didn't you tell us? No wonder you've been so distraught and feeling so sick." She mouthed a 'thank you' to Jillian for passing on this vital information and was just about to sit down with Jane to wait their turn when Imogen came running out of the room, calling for a nurse. Then she addressed her friend in an excited voice.

"Jillian! Jillian! He's waking up. His eyelids flickered and his fingers moved!"

★★★

Vincent was out of danger and everyone breathed a sigh of relief. Jane had told him that her mum and dad and his own family knew about her pregnancy and were all happy about it. Now it was time for a few more home truths. He had been out of the coma for almost a week and well on the way to making a full recovery. Keith and Robert came in together. Although Vincent had not known the other two workmen very well he was extremely upset to hear that they had died and felt so sorry for their families. And then Robert had delivered this extra bombshell, explaining that he wasn't actually his real father after all.

"So I have two dads," Vincent declared, accepting the unexpected news without histrionics, his words somewhat slurred due to the medication which was still making him feel quite groggy. "That's cool. An extra grandfather for my baby."

The two older men exchanged amused grins.

"And an extra granny," confirmed Robert.

"The more help we have, the better," Vincent wittered. "And Imogen and Jillian will both be aunts. I've always liked Imogen. I'm glad she's my sister."

He closed his eyes and went back to sleep. Keith and Robert slipped out to join their wives.

"How did he take it," Dorothy asked, concerned.

"Couldn't have gone better," Robert told her.

The two women experienced a welcome feeling of calmness.

"Let's all go and have a drink while he's asleep," Keith suggested. "I think we can put the events of the past behind us at last."

"He's banking on a bit of baby-sitting from you," Robert said to Joanna as they all made their way to the door. "This is going to be one very spoilt baby."

Joanna smiled and felt a glow of contentment. "Why don't we all go back to our place," she proposed on a whim. "I'll order up some pizzas and we can open a bottle of wine or two. Then I'll make some coffee."

There was a moment's hesitation from the other three.

"There's no need to worry," Joanna added, with a saucy grin. "I don't keep broken cups anymore."

A sharp intake of breath followed by a round of laughter heralded a long-awaited truce.

"Sounds like a plan," Dorothy declared, leading Robert by the hand. "Let's go. I'll have pepperoni and pineapple."

"Onion and chorizo for me please," answered her husband.

Keith squeezed Joanna's hand. "Is this really happening?" he said. "I can scarcely believe it."

"Isn't it wonderful!" agreed Joanna. "We have our friends back and you are finally going to get to know your son."

"Our son," Keith corrected her, planting a kiss on her cheek. "I love you, Jo."

He hadn't called her Jo for twenty-six years.

Chapter 32

Vince was out of hospital, recuperating nicely at home where he was expected to make a full recovery. Even now that the drugs had worn off he was still very blasé about the news of his unorthodox parentage and appeared to consider it as no big deal. Indeed he seemed to think that it gave him some extra leverage in explaining away Jane's unplanned pregnancy. Jillian was paying him a visit.

"I can't help thinking about those two guys who died," she told him. "It could so easily have been you."

"I know. It's scary."

"Have they found out what actually caused the explosion?"

"Faulty equipment. Looks like I'll probably be in line for some compensation."

"Quite right too after all you've been through."

"I feel bad that I wasn't able to attend the funerals."

"Their families will understand. They know how ill you've been. You need to concentrate on getting well again. You're going to need all your strength with a new baby on the way."

Vincent smiled. He was looking forward to being a dad.

Jillian heard a buzz from her phone. She fished it out from her bag and read the message.

"Strange that you were just mentioning funerals," she then told her brother. "Looks like I'll be attending one."

"Who's died?" he asked.

"It's Maggie's dad. She told me he was ill but I didn't realise that he was dying."

"Maggie?"

"A girl from work. Ben and I got to know her quite well a few months ago when we did the issue on adult literacy. She was very friendly and has kept in touch."

"What are you working on for your next edition?" Vincent asked, preferring to talk about the magazine itself rather than dwell on the death of someone he didn't even know.

Before Jillian could give him an answer she heard the doorbell ring and looked out of the window. "It's your other sister," she announced, "so I'll leave you to chat to her and go pay Maggie a visit now."

She let Imogen in and noticed that she was laden with bars of chocolate and boyish magazines.

"I could get used to this," quipped Vince.

★★★

Maggie opened the door and ushered Jillian in. "It's so kind of you to call," she said. "My head is all over the place."

"I just want to offer you my condolences," Jillian told her, handing over the bunch of yellow roses she had brought. "Were you very close to your father?"

Maggie shook her head. "No, we weren't close at all. My parents split when I was eight. I lived with my mum."

Jillian began to wonder whether she should have come. "But you did still see him?" she asked. The restaurant scene entered her mind. Just Maggie with her new fiancé and her mum. No dad. Hadn't she said he was ill?

Maggie sighed. "Yes, from time to time. But he always seemed to be in a bad mood. He never wanted to do fun things like other dads. I don't know why this has hit me so hard."

"He was still your father."

Her friend had summed up her feelings in five words. She admired the roses.

"Thanks for these. They're lovely."

There were no other flowers in sight.

Maggie led Jillian into her kitchen and turned on the kettle, inviting her to stay for coffee. There was a photograph album sitting on the small wooden table. It was open at a picture of a little girl playing in a garden with a handsome young man.

"Is that you?" Jillian asked, recognising something in the expression.

"Yes, that's me." She hesitated and then added, "With my dad."

"But you both look so happy," Jillian exclaimed, confused. "It's a lovely photo."

Tears started to trickle down Maggie's face. Jillian turned the page and there was another one of the same guy with a big smile on his face as he helped his young daughter to trundle along on a pink bicycle fitted with stabilisers. And beside it, one of a pretty young woman and a toddler sitting together on a picnic rug. It had been taken in a lovely, scenic location beside a lake. "Is that your mum?"

Maggie nodded. The snapshots were the epitome of a very normal, happy young family.

"I haven't looked at these for ages," Maggie now admitted. "I can hardly remember those days but these pictures are definitive proof we were happy once. And then it all changed. He became moody and violent. He drank and he gambled and he swore. And he was unfaithful; he cheated on my mum."

Jillian was shocked. "Did he hit you?" she asked.

"No, never. He abused himself or the house rather than us." The trickle became a torrent of tears and Maggie reached for a box of tissues. "I'm sorry," she mumbled, "I'm just at a low ebb at the moment. I've never been able to make sense of it."

"Did either of them ever re-marry?"

"No."

"And there were no other children?"

"No."

"Was he ill? What did he die of?"

"It was a direct result of his excessive drinking. But yes, he was ill in other ways too. He was depressed, suicidal even at times."

Jillian put an arm round her friend. "I'm so sorry, Maggie. You never really know what's going on in people's lives. I had no idea you had all that to contend with. You're always so positive and cheerful. I've been telling everyone about the fun I had working with you that time."

Maggie managed a smile. "Don't worry," she said. "I'll bounce back. I'm just going through a bad patch." She paused for a moment and then told Jillian some more about her experiences of growing up in a broken home.

"Some days stand out in my memory more than others. I remember coming in from school one day. I must have been about ten or eleven so Mum and I had been on our own for a couple of years. I knew he was there because I saw his car parked outside. I thought he'd come back and we'd be a proper family again. I was always dreaming about him coming back. Anyway I skipped up the driveway and opened the door, expecting him to give me a big hug. And then I heard the voices from upstairs. He was screaming at my mum, asking her for money and she was shouting back at him about how he was wasting his life. He swore at her calling her a really nasty name and then there was this huge bang. I was sure he had hit her. To be honest I thought he had killed her because the house went so quiet. I just stood trembling in the kitchen. Then mum started crying and dad said he was sorry. A minute later he walked past me without even acknowledging that I was there and barged out the back door."

"What was the bang?"

"He had put his fist through the bedroom wall. He came back a few days later to repair it."

Jillian thought it best to just listen without further interruption.

"Another memory that haunts me is the time he came to my school sports day and created a scene in front of all my friends. I tried to persuade him to take part in the parents' race but he said he didn't want to because he didn't have the right shoes on. It was only for a bit of fun and the other dads weren't wearing trainers either but when I pointed that out he went berserk and told me to stop pushing him into doing things. He didn't want to 'run a stupid race' just because he was a dad. The other kids teased me about it for days and said he was just afraid of losing. I was mortified."

Jillian drank her coffee and inwardly thanked God for her cosy life. She heard the postman putting some cards through the letter box. Maggie went into the hallway to pick them up. "People are so kind," she remarked as she opened the envelopes and read the messages of support from friends and cousins. She set them on the mantelpiece above the fireplace. "You must think I'm mad," she then mused, "mourning for someone who behaved like that. He did mellow a bit in recent years and I never stopped hoping that he might turn back into the person he had once been, the person my mother fell in love with when she was just nineteen. It was worse for her. Children are more adaptable; they get over things so much more easily. But I'll never forget the heart-breaking sound of my mother crying herself to sleep, night after night."

Maggie was still fingering a white envelope that was obviously something different, something official-looking. "This is probably another rejection letter," she sighed.

"Rejection?" quizzed Jillian.

"I've applied for a few more teaching posts. I hoped that my experience with the literacy classes and the publicity I've had since your article might stand me in good stead. The governors at my last interview certainly appeared to be impressed. They all had a copy of your magazine."

"Brilliant!" agreed Jillian with a chuckle. "That's good for my sales at least."

Maggie tore the envelope open and gasped. Then she handed it to her friend to read. "Success at last! I've got the job!" she exclaimed.

The door opened and an older version of Maggie walked in, obviously her mother. Jillian had a vague recollection of meeting her in the restaurant but the encounter had been so brief.

"It's good to see you've cheered up a bit," the older woman said as Maggie reminded her who Jillian was. Maggie told her about the job offer. "Well congratulations," her mother gushed. "It's about time you had a bit of good luck."

"I was sorry to hear about your bereavement, Mrs Redpath," Jillian said, not sure whether this was appropriate or not in the circumstances that Maggie had described, but deciding that it was nevertheless good manners.

"Thank you, Jillian, but it's Margaret, same as my

daughter," she answered. "No need for formalities. Or Greta. My friends call me Greta."

"Or we sometimes call her Marguerite for fun," quipped Maggie. "Mum was born in France."

"Really? I love France."

"I never actually lived there," Greta explained. "I was born a bit prematurely while my parents were there on holiday. Apparently I gave them a bit of a shock and forced them to change their travel plans. But I must admit I have an affinity with the country. I love going back there and I collect mementos from each trip. I have some beautiful pictures of sunflowers and lavender fields and some gorgeous pottery from Brittany and Provence." She turned to her daughter. "Just while we're talking about travelling, Maggie, I have to take a short trip over to England next week, after the funeral. I'll only be gone a few days but maybe you'd keep an eye on the house for me."

"Yes, of course," Maggie told her. "That won't be a problem. You'll be wanting to visit Granny."

"My mother-in-law isn't very mobile anymore," Greta explained to Jillian, "so she won't be able to come over." Then she addressed her daughter again. "I had some remarkably civil conversations with your father during the last few weeks. Maybe it was just because he knew he was dying but he really tried to make amends for the way he has behaved, the way he has treated us both over the years. He insisted that he never stopped loving us."

"And you believe that? He left it a bit late."

"I don't expect you to understand, Maggie, but yes, I do believe that he meant it. He spoke from the heart. If only he had opened up like that years ago, things could have been so different for all of us."

Jillian didn't want to outstay her welcome. These people had plans to make and personal things to discuss. But she was glad she had visited. And she went away feeling more grateful than ever that she had two loving parents who had brought her up on an even keel in an atmosphere of unconditional love and harmony. Even when they had made that one big transgression they had not let it ruin what they had. And the same was true for Imogen's family. The incident almost seemed quite minor now. Maggie had not been so lucky.

Chapter 33

Grant and Imogen made their engagement official at the end of the month, choosing a ring together and spending a romantic weekend at their favourite seaside retreat up north, where they wined and dined and walked for miles, taking in the stunning coastal scenery and the bracing sea air. It was a glorious end to the summer.

Now, two weeks on, Imogen was experiencing another milestone in their relationship. She was about to sleep in the marital bed that Grant had shared with Zoe. They still planned to find a new home of their own but in the meantime Imogen had accepted that Grant already had one and had decided that she had put off moving in with him for long enough. She had suggested it herself, pointing out that Vince and Jane could take over the flat. It made sense for all of them.

There was a photograph of Zoe on the bedside table, illuminated by the soft glow from the lamp. Grant had hidden it in a drawer but Imogen had found it and put it back where it belonged.

"If I died," she had reasoned with him, "I'd want you to be happy again after a while and move on with your life. But I wouldn't like to think that you'd forget me or cut me out altogether. She deserves no less."

Grant had just responded by holding her close, impressed by her level of maturity and understanding as their two hearts beat as one.

Imogen slipped in first under the crisp red duvet and nestled into the cool grey pillows, making herself comfortable against the new bedclothes they had bought together earlier in the day. Then she closed her eyes and took a deep breath and as Grant slid in beside her any worries she might have had just melted away like dew on a summer's morning. He was loving and gentle and passionate in equal measure and Imogen's heart was almost bursting with happiness. Afterwards she drifted into the most restful and dreamless sleep imaginable.

★★★

They were just finishing breakfast and discussing how to spend their first day of living under the same roof when Grant heard a buzz from his phone and checked the message.

Morning Grant. I've just had a call from your grandmother. She wants the whole family over at her place for about two o'clock this afternoon. I know it's very short notice but I hope that you and Imogen can come. She sounded very serious. I hope there's nothing wrong. Mum x

"Sorry, Sweetheart," Grant said, after reading it aloud. "Do you mind?"

"No, of course not," Imogen replied. "You've spent the last month looking out for my family. It's time yours got a look in."

"I hope she isn't ill or something," mused Grant. "It's not like her to make spur of the moment announcements. She always plans her parties well in advance."

His phone buzzed again.

Just been summoned over to Granny Gertrude's this afternoon. Jillian too. Any idea what's going on? Thomasina was very curt. Bradley

Grant read it out loud again and pulled a face. "I don't like the sound of this," he said.

They all arranged to go together; Grant would swing by the apartment and pick up Jillian and Bradley. Maybe it was just something to do with the weddings; but none of them really believed that. There was a sense of foreboding in the air and the mood was sombre. Soon they were standing on Gertrude's doorstep.

Mark opened the door and welcomed them. "I don't know what this is about any more than you do," he assured them when he saw their worried faces. "All Gertrude would tell Catherine was that she has something to say and that she doesn't want to have to say it umpteen times. That's why she wants us all here together." He led them into the sitting-room. Rebecca was already there along with Catherine, Robyn and Jack. Gertrude gave the new arrivals a few minutes to settle themselves and then she followed them in and gave a little cough to clear her throat, indicating that she was ready to make her announcement.

"Thomasina and Alastair aren't here yet," cautioned Catherine, thinking that her mother had overlooked this fact by mistake.

"I saw Aunt Thomasina's car in the driveway," observed Grant.

"Yes," Gertrude now disclosed. "They are both in the house, or out in the garden to be more accurate. They already know what I am going to tell you."

"Well, don't keep us in suspense any longer, Granny," Rebecca called out. "Why all the secrecy?"

More sure than ever now that Gertrude was going to announce that she was sick or dying, Grant gave his sister a nudge to silence her. She scowled at him in return. Everyone else experienced a feeling of apprehension.

"Thomasina had a visit from the police yesterday morning," Gertrude divulged at last.

Nine pairs of eyes stared at her, aghast.

"They gave her this letter."

She held the letter aloft so that they could all see it.

"She came straight over here and we read it together. We talked to Alastair about it last night."

Robyn said what they were all thinking. "What is it? Who's it from?"

"It's sort of anonymous," replied Gertrude. "It's addressed to the Henning family. Thomasina wants me to read it to you. She's going to send a copy to Ray's parents."

The girls remembered that Alastair's paternal grandparents lived abroad.

"Are you sure you want Jillian and me here?" Bradley interrupted. "We're not family."

"Yes, quite sure, my dear boy," Gertrude confirmed. "We all count you as one of us. And your lovely fiancée too."

Gertrude paused for a moment, bracing herself, and then began to read the letter.

To Mrs Thomasina Henning and family,

You don't know me and I had never heard of you until a few weeks ago.

I want to inform you that my former husband passed away recently. He had a difficult life and was plagued with anger issues, self-doubt and depression which only came to the fore some considerable time after our marriage. On two occasions he actually attempted suicide. I could never understand what had changed him because the man I had married had appeared to be perfectly happy and well-adjusted at the time. I blamed myself thinking that he didn't love me after all and must have felt trapped. We got divorced a long time ago but stayed in touch due to us having a daughter together.

When he was dying he made a shocking confession to me and suddenly it all made sense. He had apparently been struggling with guilt and remorse ever since the accident that claimed the life of your husband back in 1990. He told me that he had been rushing for the ferry that night because he had a meeting to attend here in England the following day. He said he knew he had hit someone but he swore that he didn't realise how bad it was and he just drove on. Two weeks later he read a report about the incident in a newspaper. It was only then that he realised the man had died. He never told me or anyone else about it but it's clear now that it was always on his mind. He changed from that day on.

He asked me to write this letter to you. He is not asking for your forgiveness but just wanted you to know that the person who destroyed your life is now dead. I wish that he had admitted his guilt at the time. He could have been given an appropriate punishment and then you and maybe we too could have drawn a line under it. Instead he gave himself a life sentence and died a very unhappy man.

I noticed in the newspaper report (my

husband kept it and showed it to me) that you had a son who was also injured. He said that he never heard any more about the boy so I am assuming and hoping that he made a full recovery. I am so sorry that he had to grow up without his father.

I hope that you will understand my decision to remain anonymous. I just want to move on and maybe even find love again, now that I know the failure of our marriage was not actually down to me. I hope this also gives you some kind of closure.

With my very best wishes,
Marguerite

Everyone sat stock still as Gertrude finished reading. Imogen's heart was thumping ten to the dozen as she recalled those diary entries that had caused her to suspect her own parents of being involved in Alastair's accident. This letter would have proved their innocence and all that embarrassment over what had really taken place could have been avoided. But then she would not have found her brother. Grant sensed her discomfort and gave her hand a supportive squeeze. Jillian, meanwhile, was reeling with shock. Marguerite! She could hardly take it in. That poor man. This was one secret she would have to keep to the grave. No-one spoke.

And then suddenly they were all speaking at once and exploding with rage.

"What a coward!"

"Is this woman for real! How dare she try to evoke our sympathies for her own miserable existence."

"So a slap on the wrist would have made everything OK! They could have resumed their happy marriage and would have conveniently forgotten about us."

"She doesn't even know what happened to Alastair, hasn't bothered to find out."

Rebecca was livid. "That man has lived and died with his good name intact. That's not right. People should know what he did. I'm going to track this woman down. There can't be too many people called Marguerite who recently buried an ex-husband. What else do we know about her? They had a daughter. He had work contacts in England. Do ferry companies keep records from as far back as that? I mean, this all happened before I was even born."

"Probably not," put in Bradley. "And she's probably not called Marguerite at all."

Jillian felt the panic rising, the blood rushing to her head.

"It might not even be true," agreed Grant. "An anonymous letter cannot be taken as concrete evidence of anything."

"If it is true, he deserved his wretched life," Robyn said. "And she shouldn't be making excuses for him. It just makes her as bad as he was."

Thomasina had slipped in from the garden, unnoticed. She was standing by Gertrude's side, listening to the angry comments. Gertrude hadn't said anything since reading the letter itself. Now she spoke for both of them.

"I don't think we should be uncharitable or vindictive," she cautioned. "The police do think that the letter is genuine. It was posted in England and the envelope they received also included the newspaper article she mentioned and a couple of other details which give her story authenticity. They do believe, however, that it is more likely than not that she has made up the name."

"I don't think that she is making excuses for him," Thomasina put in. "He ruined her life as well as ours. Not to mention his own. I respect her for getting in touch with us and putting us in the picture. I think we should accept this at face value and let it go."

"Whatever you say, Thomasina," Catherine affirmed. "Raymond was your husband. It's your decision."

"And Alastair's father. Alastair agrees with me."

"Then who are we to interfere?" proclaimed Mark, standing up to signify the end of the discussion. "Let's all get out into the garden. It's a beautiful day out there."

Jillian breathed a huge sigh of relief.

As they filed out Gertrude took Imogen aside and thanked her for coming. "I'm sure that wasn't easy for you," she whispered. "But just to let you know, I haven't said anything to the girls about what transpired in the restaurant that night so nobody knows about it." Imogen gave her a grateful smile.

"What are you two whispering about?" quizzed Thomasina.

"Just telling Imogen that I'm glad she is moving in with Grant," Gertrude bluffed. "The sooner the better."

"Actually I already did," revealed Imogen. "Yesterday."

"Oh, that's great news."

"It is indeed," agreed Thomasina, giving her nephew's fiancée a warm hug before heading outside to join the others.

"It was lovely meeting your parents that night," Gertrude added. "I'm glad your brother is OK now."

Grant came back in some minutes later looking for Imogen and found her still in conversation with his grandmother. He smiled. "It's good to see that you two have become as thick as thieves," he chuckled. "No wonder they named a couple of storms after you last winter. You're both a force to be reckoned with. But you're missing all the excitement outside."

Imogen took his outstretched hand and followed him through the kitchen and out into the warm sunshine. There was indeed an air of jollity and Champagne corks were being popped.

"What's the occasion?" Imogen asked. She hoped they weren't celebrating that man's death. No matter what he had done, it struck her that such a show of revelry would be tasteless in the extreme. But she needn't have worried. It was nothing to do with that.

"Bradley has asked Alastair to be Best Man at his wedding," Grant told her. "He's over the moon."

"You have no idea what this will mean to him," Thomasina gushed, having overheard their conversation. "Alastair has had to get used to being left out of things over the years. He has always been seen as different, slow and even stupid in so many people's eyes with folk who should know better treating him like an outcast. This will do wonders for his self-esteem."

"I hope she doesn't mean me," Grant mumbled, as he backed away still holding on to Imogen's hand and reflecting on his aunt's words.

"Of course she doesn't!" Imogen reassured him. "But you're family. It comes naturally to you to be supportive. Bradley chose to be a friend. I think it's wonderful."

"Sorry," he ventured. "It's just a remnant of that childhood jealousy still niggling away at my brain."

"Don't forget it was Bradley who brought us together. If it wasn't for him I'd still be thinking you were a lecherous, cheating bastard."

That brought a smile to his face. "That's true," he admitted.

"Who did you have as Best Man when you married Zoe?" Imogen now asked.

"Nigel."

"And will you ask him again?"

Grant sighed. "To tell you the truth, I'd love to just go away for the weekend and come back married without any fuss or ceremony."

"Done!" Imogen's face lit up. "There's nothing I'd like more."

"Seriously?"

"Absolutely! I hate big weddings."

Jillian brought them both a celebratory drink. "What a year it's been," she exclaimed with a radiant smile. She had regained her composure and had decided to cast what she had learnt today from her mind. Thank God Bradley hadn't come with her when she visited Maggie. Or Imogen for that matter. "None of this would have been happening if we hadn't moved into that flat together. We would never have met this lovely family." Bradley and Alastair joined them with their own glasses.

"Nice one, Brad," Grant exclaimed, feeling magnanimous after the exchange with his fiancée. "That has certainly gone down well with the rellies." Then he turned to his cousin and congratulated him. Alastair beamed with pride as Imogen tapped him on the arm and said that she couldn't wait to see him all dressed up.

Grant took a sip of his Champagne and then ran his finger over the rim of the flute. "I'll just go and get another glass," he said. "This one is chipped."

Before he could move the two girls burst out laughing as a recent heart-to-heart with their parents came to mind. All three men were baffled. "What's so funny?" asked Alastair.

"Search me!" exclaimed Grant.

"No idea," Bradley agreed.

"Just go and get yourself another drink," Imogen said with a lightness of heart that only Jillian fully understood. "And throw away all your chipped glasses and broken cups. They can be dangerous, you know."

"Very dangerous!" Jillian concurred, still laughing. "You won't find any of those in my house."

"You two are mad," remarked Alastair with a twinkle in his eye.

They both gave him a hug as Gertrude's voice rang

out from just behind them and Grant hurried in to get a fresh drink.

"I would like to return to the purpose of our coming together this afternoon and propose a toast," she said, raising her glass. "To Marguerite, whoever she is. I hope she finds peace."

"Marguerite," chorused a dozen voices, accepting Gertrude's benevolence and following her lead. Jillian's eyes filled up with unshed tears.

"And another toast," Alastair suggested hesitantly.

They all looked at him in amazement; he very rarely spoke out in public.

"To the best granny in the world," he said.

As the sound of her name echoed around the garden in the hot afternoon sun, Gertrude looked on with pride and joy. Her grandson was coming out of his shell and obviously approved of the stance she had taken. He was going to be OK.

Catherine sidled over to her son. "I had a visit from Patty last night," she told him. She took an envelope out of her pocket. "She asked me to pass this on to you. It's from Cameron."

Grant was shocked. "I don't want it," he declared.

Catherine gave it to him anyway, remembering that Imogen had reported a similar reaction when she had given him her own letter. He had very quickly changed his mind on that occasion and had jetted off to Edinburgh within days. She turned to walk away.

"I don't want it," he repeated, more vehemently this time.

Imogen stood awkwardly beside him. This had to be

Grant's own decision. She didn't want to influence him one way or the other. Bradley and Jillian diplomatically strolled over to chat to Rebecca, taking Alastair with them. Grant turned the envelope over a few times in his hands and then very deliberately marched towards the summer house and took a box of matches from a drawer. He came back out and threw the envelope into the barbecue which was sitting on the patio, empty except for a thin layer of dust and ashes which had been left to cool after yesterday's meal. He struck a match and watched as the communication from his father went up in flames. Then he made it clear that he was just burning a piece of rubbish and didn't want to hear another word about it.

The party continued for another hour.

"I'll make it up to you next week," Grant whispered to Imogen. "It's not how I envisaged spending our first day together."

"Are you joking?" she replied. "I've had a brilliant day."

"Let's go home." He was looking a bit randy as he caressed her face and stroked her hair.

"Yes, let's go," she agreed. "I need to check all the cupboards while it's fresh in my mind."

"Check the cupboards?" he quizzed. "What for?"

"Broken cups of course."

Grant scratched his head and looked puzzled. "Am I missing something here?" he asked.

Jillian overheard the exchange and grinned at her friend. "Did you ever imagine we'd be able to laugh about it?" she said with a chuckle.

Grant and Bradley just looked at each other and shook their heads, as the four of them piled into the car.

"I'll drive," Imogen whispered in Grant's ear. "I only had a few sips of Champagne."

"I noticed that," Grant whispered back. "Are you feeling OK?"

"Never better."

"You normally enjoy a glass or two."

"Just thought maybe I shouldn't."

"You don't mean …"

"I think I do."

"Really?"

"I'm pretty sure."

"What are you two whispering about in the front there?"

"Just saying what a great day it's been," Imogen bluffed, smiling at Grant.

"It's been wonderful," Jillian agreed. "I was so proud of Bradley."

"Me too," Grant echoed. "You've been a real brick to my cousin over the years, Mate. I don't say it often enough but the world could do with more people like you."

Bradley gulped. *Wow! Praise from Grant.* "You two want to join us for a bite to eat?" he asked, feeling elated.

Grant just wanted to go home, to be alone with the girl he loved, the girl who was going to marry him during a romantic weekend break just as soon as they could get it arranged, the girl who was now expecting his baby and whose beautiful blue eyes were smiling at him, full of love and desire.

"Not tonight," he told his friends. "Let's make it a date for next week. For now, I'm going home to help Imogen count cups or something."

"I'll go for the 'or something'," Imogen intimated with a beguiling glance. "The cups can wait."

"Suits me," Grant answered with a grin. "Suits me just fine."

Epilogue

Patricia Campbell was just getting into bed when her mobile started to ring on her bedside table. Her husband looked up from his book. "Who's ringing you at this late hour?" he asked, a little concerned. "I hope there's nothing wrong with any of the children."

"It's just Cathy," she bluffed, seeing Douglas McKendrick's name in the caller display. "I'll take it downstairs so that we don't disturb you."

She raced down to the kitchen and closed the door behind her. The phone had stopped ringing so she selected the call back function and waited to hear the voice of her lover.

"Patty?"

"Yes, of course it's me," she hissed. "What on earth are you calling me for at this time of day? My phone was sitting right beside Kenneth. We're lucky he didn't pick it up."

"Sorry."

"What's so urgent?"

"I miss you. When are you coming over?"

"Soon. Maybe next weekend."

"Oh, that's wonderful, Darling. I can't wait to see you."

"Me too. Is that really why you called me?"

"No," Douglas now admitted. "I'm calling on behalf of my old friend, Cam Ferguson. It's about that letter he asked me to pass on to you."

"The letter for Grant Cartwright?"

"Yes. Did you know that they are father and son?"

"I guessed as much years ago," Patty revealed, "but Cathy would never own up to it. I don't see so much of her these days. She's happily married now and I don't think she approves of my lifestyle or my relationship with you. In fact I think she blames me for leading her astray in the past."

"But you do still see her?" Douglas was momentarily worried. "You will give her that letter for Grant?"

"You sound very serious all of a sudden. Is it that important?"

"Apparently it is. He contacted me again today to check whether I had passed it on yet. He sounded extremely anxious and I got the impression that there was some urgency about it. I promised him that I would remind you to deliver it."

"Well, you can tell him not to worry on that score," Patty avowed. "I gave the letter to Cathy last night and she told me that she would definitely be seeing Grant today so Mr Ferguson can rest assured that whatever is so important is already in his son's possession. Now, I'm away back to bed before Kenneth gets suspicious and comes looking for me."

"OK, thanks Patty. That will put Cam's mind at rest. See you next week. I love you. Sleep well."

"You too, Dougie. I wish now that I'd read that letter myself before handing it over. Sounds very intriguing."

"I was thinking the same thing. Guess we'll never know what was so important about it. But at least we played our part in getting it delivered to the young man safe and sound. I liked the guy."

"It wasn't a problem. What are friends for?"

"Night, Sweetheart."

"Night, Dougie. Sweet dreams."